Kilmarii
The Wayfinder

Lisa Newton

Original Book Cover Art by Sage Lee

Sage Lee is an undergraduate student at Parsons School of Design in New York City. Sage Lee is currently studying Fashion Design. Sage is based in Glastonbury, Connecticut, and is experienced in fashion and illustration related commissions. @sillillillie on Instagram.

Crystal Heart Imprints
Springfield, Illinois
Printed in the USA

Dedication

Mrs. Edwards, Mary Greene, Ruth Souther
Thank you for believing in my writing voice.

Rebecca Davidson, Tim Kinsella, Dinara Newton
Karyn Perry, Carmen Rivera
Thank you for your wise words.

Stephanie Urbina Jones & Jeremy Pager
Thank you for helping me recapture my dreams.

Family Relationships

Human Knowers, Siblings
Tozi, Mato, Jyukan, Ouray
Kayko, Jyukan's son

Maleia & Mato's Daughters
Malka, Lanika, Layloni

Siblings by Adoption
Pare, Tessi, Kryn

Asil Wysong, Yuki Descendant

Whale Names
Yachai, Kaiyah, Sedna Wanahi

Contents

Kilmarii The Wayfinder

The Story Begins

The University of Arizona, U.S.A.

"The sound of the waves was faint in the crisp, coolness of the still night air. The hulls of the ships rocked and bobbed, mere specks on the vastness of the Pacific Ocean. Off in the distance, still a full day's sail away, floated a simple raft carrying an extraordinary girl."

Asil shifted, adjusted her long black skirt, and pushed her glasses back up the bridge of her nose. She habitually moved her white braid, adorned with silver and turquoise, in front of her shoulder. Her multitude of rings flinted in the spotlight as her hands spoke at the same rate as her words.

She was comfortable in front of any audience. In fact, it was her happy place. And with her teacher's hands weaving an invisible tapestry of words into the air, she rose from her stool and began to pace the stage.

"This is the story, as told over many generations. I am Asil Wysong, the direct descendant of the Yutki clan. I am the current keeper of our stories and your guest speaker for tonight.

"Whenever possible, I will use the names of places and things as they are known in our time, but keep in mind that sea levels and the climate zones were dramatically different back then, and there was no written language to confirm what has been passed down from one story keeper to another. These are the oral histories of my ancient ancestors."

The auditorium lights dimmed. Oh, how she loved the drama of it all. The spotlight widened, and Asil slowly strolled to the opposite side of the stage, as she mentally prepared.

"Long ago, before the great earthquakes and fire rained down from the sky, when glyptodon armadillo worked alongside the Nek, the giant fanged cats hunted the bison, the Nanoladon Pacifica whales dominated the coast and were the partners, the Yutki clan came to be.

"Our creation grew out of the ocean, our secrets discovered across the land. We are a clan of three worlds: the below, the above, and the within. This is the story of the below, the world that was built from the water."

She looked out into her captive audience of university students, tilted her head slightly, placed

Kilmarii The Wayfinder

her hands palm up, and stated, "Basically, during the Neolithic era in what we know now as Central and Northern America."

Chapter One

The First Yutki Warrior

Below the ocean's surface, the whales began their nightly sounding, the unison cries of exhaustion and impatience, as they had grown resentful of their harnesses that kept them from doing anything more than surfacing for air.

The whale ships would only continue to grow heavier as the journey continued. The calf growing inside Kaiyah had to be born in the warm waters, and this instinctively drove them forward.

It would be the first calf born to the Esor people, in the time of the rise of the Yutki clan. All members of the clan, whale and human, waited for the first sounds to emanate.

It was the job of the Yutkis to calm the whales and maintain them in their harnesses until safely in the warm waters of the whale nursery, still two moons away. The sound of the waves grew faint in the crisp, coolness of the still night air. The hulls of the ships wove seamlessly behind the wake of the whales. The four ships were mere specks on the black vastness of the Pacific.

Maleia and Jyukan had climbed the mast ropes and sat together at the top, surveying the distance around the ships. Mapping the locations of the stars, they were pleased with their course on the second journey to Teotihuacan. Using their hand signals, they instructed the Yutkis to prepare to dive under their ships to inspect their whales for injuries and to comfort them.

Matching the unison of the whales' calls, the Yutkis led the clan in the chant that signaled to the whales it was time to stop. All members of the clan pounded their fists and stomped their feet until the hulls of the ship sent their sound waves like giant drums to the ears of the whales.

Maleia and Jyukan guided the clan to the resting stop on the western side of Mount Shasta Peninsula. For the next two days, the clan would hunt sea lions, otters, octopus, trap seabirds, and net fish. They would harvest abalone, starfish, and seaweed to preserve for the trade market in Teotihuacan.

From the railing of the first ship, Kayko watched the Yutkis dive under. He was the youngest son of Jyukan, and like his father, his ability was strong. When they returned to their summer grounds, he would begin his Yutki training. On that day, he was watching to learn. The sea was black, too dark to see what was happening below.

Kayko scanned the surface for his favorite whale, Yachai. His mother and father had once been her caretakers. And it was she who intervened when his mother was attacked by the sharks. Kayko used his ability to communicate mentally with all animals to greet Yachai.

Yachai responded by sending him a memory vision of them rising through a sea of air bubbles, as she breached, flinging him from his fin perch out in front of her.

Kayko remembered squealing with delight as the whale nudged him gently with its closed mouth. With a playful flick of its head, the whale had launched him upward, sending him soaring into the air.

He remembered how he had felt floating in the air until he plummeted into the dark ocean. With a splash, he hit the surface, his laughter bubbling up as he bobbed above the gentle waves.

Before he could catch his breath, Yachai was beneath him, rising smoothly, and throwing him again, lifting him effortlessly out of the water. Up he'd go, then down again in another joyful descent.

Each time, Yachai timed the playful launches perfectly, always ensuring Kayko's safe return to the sea. The child's laughter echoed over the water, infectious and full of glee. The two continued as an unspoken bond formed between them in this shared joy.

Kilmarii The Wayfinder

"Again, Yachai! Again!" young Kayko had joyfully called out.

And she continued many times until Kayko was so exhausted that he was unable to swim safely. Kayko also remembered how Jyukan had swum to him and together they had wept, wrapped in each other's arms in the privacy of their shattered hearts.

The memory caused his heart to race beneath his chest.

The matriarch whale, Yachai, no longer birthed new calves, as she was older than all could remember. Kayko was forbidden to dive to her again until he finished Yutki school, but he must answer her.

Closing his eyes, he inhaled deeply, and Kayko strengthened Yachai's memory vision by adding his own memories to the stream. They were linked once more in the waters when she had swum with him. From that moment, their hearts became one, as she would always hold the spirit of his mother's memory.

Are you hungry? Kayko asked Yachai.

I do not need to eat during this season.

This was not the answer he had expected, so he asked, *When will you eat again?*

I will eat in the nursery and then not again until we reach our home hunting waters. Kaiyah, Wanahi, and Sedna may eat during the hunt.

Kayko continued to ask Yachai questions, *Do you have a mate?*

I no longer wish to mate.

Are Wanahi, Sedna, and Kaiyah your children?
Kaiyah is my child.
Where did Wanahi and Sedna come from?
Maleia called for them to come to us during a storm. When the storm was over, their whale family had gone out to the deep ocean. They listen for them, but they have never returned for them.

Kayko could relate, as he also listened for his mother to return to him.

The Story of Maleia and Mato

Maleia scanned the minds of the whales systematically. She recognized Yachai's and Kayko's bond and saw their conversation through the whale's mind projections. She watched keenly to see if Kayko would join her or not in the water. It was important to know if Kayko could be trusted to follow her directives.

She was the leader of the Yutkis and the most powerful whale and animal seer the clan had ever known.

Maleia was found living in a sea cave by Tozi, the Esor medicine woman. Mato had noticed Maleia in the home of his sister, Tozi, while on the winter hunting expedition. He had observed her skillfully ice fishing with a hatchet and spear.

Her heavy, dark hair fell past her hips. Her muscular legs seemed oblivious to the cold. Every time she broke the ice and threw her spear, a fish was impaled on the other end. Never had he witnessed such skill. He inquired who she was, as he had no recollection of her as a member of the clan.

Tozi projected the mental answer to the question she found in her brother's mind.

She talks with the fish. I found her living where the river meets the ocean.

Who are her people?

We don't know. She does not speak of them. Tozi continued, *She does not speak a known language, and she seldom uses her voice. However, she did draw this.*

Tozi unfolded a large seal skin that held a detailed map that included pictures of plants, animals, and a particular temple Mato recognized. She placed her outstretched finger on that location far to the south.

Is this where she is from? Mato asked, in great admiration, as he watched the woman pull large fish out from the frozen lake. It was clear she knew exactly where to break the ice to spear the fish.

I would say that is where she wants to go.

As he contemplated how this fish-seer woman would be valuable on the big river, his mind drew an image of her from a different angle; a moose was charging her. Seeing through the moose's eyes, Mato took aim at the animal and let loose his arrow from the bow. The arrow flew over Maleia's left shoulder and embedded deeply into the throat of the moose. The silence of the arrow was matched by the loud thud of the animal hitting the ground.

Maleia faced Mato and raised her spear above her head, then lowered it. She had met an equal. She walked over to face him.

Maleia spoke directly to Mato. Her fierce tone caused Tozi to choke back a startled breath of shock.

"Who are you?"

Mato instinctively addressed her in a formal manner reserved for addressing a fellow warrior, "I thought you did not speak our language."

"I learned. Who are you?"

"I am Mato, brother of Tozi the medicine woman, brother of Jyukan and Ouray the Nek."

Without warning, Maleia braced Mato's jaw in her hand, then slowly circled around, letting her hand travel across his shoulders, the spread of his back, and rest on his hip. She drew her eyes up to his. She did not possess the skill of being able to scan his thoughts, but she could read his desires as he reacted to her. Yes, she liked this one. This one was interesting.

"What do you think you are doing, Maleia? You may not touch Mato."

Tozi spoke sharply, as she looked around nervously, hoping no one else in the settlement had seen this transgression.

Mato did not move. His eyes were transfixed and lost inside Maleia's. His hands instinctively drew her close to his body. Although tempted, he did not read her mind, for he preferred to learn more about her over the natural passage of time.

"Maleia, did you not know the moose was charging you?"

Indignation swelled up from her chest and out of her mouth, "My spear was ready."

"You were going to kill a moose with your spear?"

Raising her hatchet, "...and my acuax."

"Hatchet."

Mato pointed to each as he repeated the words in a patronizing tone.

"Spear and hatchet."

He now looked at her closely. She bared scars of untold battles across her arms and legs. He wondered what the rest of her body looked like.

Some clan women arrived and carried away the fish and the moose to prepare them.

Mato turned to Tozi and nodded in respect.

"I will return to my hunt."

"I will join you."

"Women are not permitted to hunt."

The indignation flowed out into Maleia's response, "I speared all these fish. This is hunt."

"Fishing is not dangerous."

She wanted to wipe the righteous smirk off Mato's face.

Maleia struggled to retort in her newly acquired language, "You not hunt ocean."

Maleia picked up immediately on a silent exchange between Mato and Tozi. Her gut told her that it was true that this clan did not hunt in the ocean. The revelation explained why Tozi had brought her up into the highlands. The anger stirring in her throat was replaced by a smile lighting up her eyes. This was what she would teach these people, and in return, she would claim this man, Mato. For Maleia, this was decided.

Mato realized this strange warrior woman knew methods of hunting in the ocean, for he could not resist gathering the images from her memories as she walked around him so boldly. Greatly impressed, he was anxious to share this news with his father.

"When I return from the hunt, I will take you to my father at the end of the great river, where it meets the ocean, and organize a fish hunt. You can demonstrate how you hunt then. You cannot join us now."

Maleia's hatchet landed squarely in the middle of the tree trunk beside Mato's head. She pivoted on her heel and ducked inside Tozi's doorway.

"When did you find your voice?" Tozi snapped at her.

"What does it matter? It is here now."

Tozi's home felt too small for both women to occupy at that moment.

"Know your place, Maleia, or I will toss you back into the ocean waters from which you came."

Maleia did not acknowledge the threat, but instead she asked, "And what place does Mato have?"

Kilmarii The Wayfinder

At this point, Tozi had enough of her rudeness. She delved inside the mind of Maleia to gather the insights she needed to make sense of this impetuous woman.

"He is born of the leaders of the Esor people, and he is my brother."

"And you? Who are you, Tozi?" Maleia practically spat out her misdirected anger.

"This you already know. What is your real question?"

"Is Mato mated?"

Tozi roared with laughter. Embarrassed, but soon thereafter, Maleia was overcome with laughter, too. And the true bond of friendship took root between Tozi and Maleia.

And in time, Maleia was not only accepted by the Esor clan as a warrior and hunter but also joined in a love union with Mato.

Their union grew so strong that Maleia only had children with Mato. They created three daughters, each of whom had her powers over fish and animals, but none had the power of their father to read humans.

Due to Mato's superiority, the clan members afforded him the final word, yet in his relationship with Maleia, they were equals.

Mato took great pride in the fact that Maleia had brought the knowledge of the whales into the clan and trained the first whale seers. It was she who had shown Mato how to make the harnesses out of seal skins.

And it was she who taught the Esors how to fish using dolphins, whales, and large gill nets. It was Mato and Maleia who envisioned and built the settlement where the great river met the ocean, and designed the ships that the whales pulled.

Within two seasons of the union of Mato to Maleia, four whale ships were built by the Nek, and a permanent settlement was established on top of the cliffs at the mouth of the Columbia River. Maleia and Mato maintained a residence along the shoreline where the whales and ships were protected. The rest of the Esor people remained further inland and rotated between the hunting camps in the highlands.

The number of Esor people staying at the mouth of the river increased as Maleia began what she called the Yutki hunters. In the tradition of the clan, children learned the trade of their parents.

However, Maleia broke with tradition with her insistence on exclusivity of choosing the few Esor children who were, like her, both fish and animal seers. To further strengthen her own position and separate the chosen children from their Esor families, Maleia taught the chosen children her language for all Yutki communication.

This strategy eventually gave her unprecedented control over these children, which drove a wedge of discourse amongst the Esor families.

The Esor elders held a council meeting to discuss the discord and express their concern about the outsider's rise in power. The tribal elders, Mik and elder Mato, decided to create a separate ocean cliff settlement for the Yutki people and their families, and placed Mato and Tozi as the elders of this Yutki settlement. And with this decision, Maleia was seen as neutralized by those who had felt threatened by her rise in power.

It was during the time Maleia was pregnant with her first child that she called for the first trading voyage to Teotihuacan. Although she remained behind with the whale ships and did not enter into trade at Teotihuacan, she was credited with the success of their first trading voyage.

From Teotihuacan, the people brought back to the Esor and Yutki settlements the knowledge and tools needed to create irrigation fields to grow crops of squash, corn, and beans. They also brought back methods for growing new root vegetables that stored well.

The establishment of these new crops and the watering circle system was transformative for the clan, so great that Maleia's previous reputation was forgotten. She was raised to elder status alongside Mato and Tozi in the Yutki settlement.

Where Mato had been a devoted and strong parent to their three daughters, Maleia was detached and kept her children under the care of others. This was her way. Maleia showed more affection to her hunting dogs than she did for her girls.

With each great accomplishment, time passed, and, one day, Mato died of old age.

Mato's death was felt by his children, as well as every person, and animal of the clan, not because he was the elder, but because he was so deeply loved and respected. However, no one mourned more deeply than Maleia.

When Mato died, Maleia's long hair was already turning white with age, and knowing that he was able to read her every thought, she continued to silently speak to him in death. Her pain was heard in the minds and hearts of the four remaining human thought readers of the clan - Tozi, Jyukan, Kayko, and Ouray. They also held the ability to read the thoughts and emotions of the people near them, similar to how the rest of the people could read animals.

Maleia's heartfelt pleas to Mato to return to her were so palpable that Jyukan offered himself to ease her suffering. She accepted him as her Yutki partner, yet nothing more would grow from this arrangement. Together, she and Jyukan were accepted as leaders of the clan.

Chapter Two

University of ArizonaProfessor Asil Wysong

Asil Wysong held up her hand, as if to signal for a restaurant to bring her the bill, and the audience lights brightened.

She took an exaggerated step to the side, extended her left arm with her water bottle precariously dangling from pinched fingers around the cap. She flipped it in the air and caught it with the same hand.

Experience had taught her that entertaining the audience with a bit of odd humor relieved any of her nervousness and doubled as a way to regain any audience members who may be losing focus.

She smiled, "Let's step aside and explain a few terms and make some clarifications."

"I have drawn up the lights to take some time to clear up a few things the audience may be questioning at this point."

"On each ship, there are Yutki, Nek, and Esor members of the clan in specific roles. Esors are the origin people, the ancestor clan. All people of that period in the Esor clan had been animal seers and, therefore, outstanding hunters. Just imagine the advantage one would have in being able to see into the mind of an animal. Neks are born within the Esors. They are children who uniquely interact with the world on their terms. Neks are specialists and inventors, and I like to think of them as the engineers of this time. Esors were both guardians and facilitators of the Neks, because often the gifts of the Neks were paired with them living in their own unique sense of time and space."

Asil put down her water on the floor and rested a hand on the top of the stool.

"All clan members who are also water animal seers would have been selected by Maleia to become Yutki. The Yutki clan members lived in a settlement next to the ocean, where they would fish, hunt in the ocean, and care for the four clan whales. The incorporation of the Yutki language as part of the permanent ocean settlement began the creation of the Yutki clan, of which I am a direct descendant."

Returning to the center of the stage, Asil adjusted the large crossbody cloth purse she had been wearing and pulled out a pair of extra-large gold hammered earrings that looked like scrolls of paper. She hooked one over the outside of her left ear and then repeated the process on the right ear.

"These earrings were handed down to me, and are designed to block human knowers from reading my mind. Similar earrings can be found in the Archeology Museum in Dublin, Ireland, in Mexico City, and Cairo, Egypt. I unfortunately did not inherit the ability to read people's minds, but just on the off chance there are any of you in the audience that can, I will keep these on."

A few brief chuckles rang out from the audience.

"We resume our story as the Yutkis are beginning another trading voyage to what we now know as Central America. Maleia and Mato's siblings (Jyukan, Tozi, and Ouray), the daughters of Maleia, and the son of Jyukan are leading the four whale ships down the Pacific coast of North America."

She resumed her storytelling.

Chapter Three

Gathering Supplies for the Voyage

The first day of the hunt, the wind had shifted and came from the northwest. The promise of rain to fill the ship's freshwater catch was well received.

The small vessels, laden with nets and traps, were clanking to the sides of the whale ships. The processing campsite being built on the beach was being supervised by Ouray, brother of Mato, and leader of the Neks.

With Ouray was Kef, his working glyptodon, a giant herbivorous armadillo, who acted not only as a counterbalance to lift heavy loads but also as Ouray's legs. Together with a multitude of clan members, they worked through the night erecting shelters and smokers, creating fire pits and pelt

Kilmarii The Wayfinder

stations, and finding a freshwater source.

Kef's wide arching back and strong bone plates easily supported Ouray and the water bladders. Once the camp was complete, Ouray and Kef would secure enough water into the ship catches to support eighty people, twelve canines, two brown eagles, a wild bunch of turkeys, and, of course, Kef.

Chapter Four

Jyukan and Kayko

Sleep evaded Jyukan. He rose quietly and climbed the ladder up to the deck. A knot rested at the back of his throat, struggling to come to the surface as a primal scream of pain.

His mind was trapped in the pain. The scars on his forearms and calf, from the shark attack, memorialized the memory of Kayko's mother's body being torn apart by the sharks.

He watched the camp being set up for a long while, then vomited over the side.

The sharks would come; they always came during the big hunts, attracted by the blood in the water. They were the creatures no animal or fish seer could know. They were stealthy killers, for no one could anticipate their actions or know they were nearby. Not even the great Maleia could read sharks.

His worries centered on Kayko, his only child, who would soon swim with a spear, monitoring against sharks. Jyukan rubbed his face and felt his advanced age. Where once it had been his job to protect the clan from shark attacks, his days were now spent guiding others from high on the mast. Resigned to the fate of it all, Jyukan remained on deck waiting for the sun to rise over the cliffs of the bay.

The sky turned dark, full of clouds heavy with rain. The ocean surface was choppy, making visibility difficult for the human eye, yet it made no difference to the whales, Kaiyah and Yachai, who were anticipating being soon detached from their ships to help the clan catch fish. Just like in the waters of home, they would swim freely in the bay, echolocate schools of fish, and drive them to the large nets spread between the small boats.

Kayko met with his cousins on deck.

"Don't disappoint us, Kayko." Malka, the first daughter of Maleia, did not hide her disdain as she sneered at her cousin.

"Are you worried Kayko will spear more fish than you?" snickered Lanikai, Kayko's secret Yutki teacher and middle daughter of Maleia.

Kayko was used to this type of banter from his cousins, especially Malka, who he suspected saw him as a potential threat once his training was completed. And that was exactly what he planned to be. After all, he was also a human knower, which gave him a great advantage over his cousins.

Lanikai gave Kayko a side hug and smiled, "Let's check in with Yachai."

After reassurances from the whale, Yachai, that she sensed no danger, they dove under the ship and released her harness. Yachai surfaced briefly, then dived straight down. Within moments, she had crested above the water surface and slammed back down close to the small vessels, causing them to nearly capsize. Kaiyah surfaced nearby. The air was filled with the excitement of the hunt.

Just as in the hunts at home, specific roles were assigned. First, the whales were unhooked from their harnesses by the Yutkis, who would then spend the rest of the time watching for sharks and relaying the whale information to the Esors who managed the nets, and to the Neks who managed the processing of the catch.

Kayko and Lanikai dove to Yachai.

Kayko rubbed his hand near the whale's giant eye, "Are you ready for the fish hunt, Yachai?"

I am ready, Lanikai and Kayko, Yachai replied. She filled Kayko's and Lanikai's minds with the image of her swimming freely in the ocean.

The released whales immediately swam in the opposite direction in earnest, looking for a large school of fish to push toward the nets.

The images from Yachai and Kaiyah were relayed to the fish hunters. Kaiyah had already found a large school of herring and was pushing it toward the middle of the bay. Yachai swam to flank the school to prevent it from spreading out, and together the two whales drove the herring to the waiting nets. Suddenly, Yachai saw a shark crossing through the middle of the school, spiraling with its mouth open.

She sent the image warning out to all who could connect with her mind stream.

"Shark in the fish!" Maleia sent out from both her mind to the eagles to disseminate and by mouth to all that could hear.

As the large swarm of silver fish approached the net, the shark attempted to swim under a vessel and was caught by its gills in the fishing net. The screaming of the fish deafened the communication between the clan members, taking away any advantage. Everyone was on their own to do their job.

Lanikai nudged Kayko and gestured for them to climb back on the ship.

The small fishing vessels closed in around the fish school, trapping the thrashing shark in the tightening torrent of panicked herring. The nets were heavy with fish, and the movement of the shark broke a wide hole in the straining net. With its gills trapped. the shark failed to escape.

From her position on the mast, Maleia watched her daughters, Malka and Kayloni swim towards the net breach.

Malka slashed at the shark's gills while Kayloni pushed her spear through the shark's eye.

The shark was motionless as its blood swirled

like smoke in the churning water.

Jyukan picked up on the whale warnings from Yachai and Kaiyah of the usually solitary sharks arriving en masse to the bay. He scanned what the eagles were seeing. He contacted Ouray and Kayko to help him relay a message to the clan members in the fishing vessels and at the shore camp.

"Pull the fish to shore."

"Everyone out of the water."

"Pull the fish to shore."

"Everyone out of the water."

"Pull the fish to shore."

From her position high on the mast of her whale ship, Maleia called to the freed whales to protect themselves and return to the ships only when it was safe.

Instinctively, the Yutkis took their posts to guard the two harnessed whales, Wanahi and Sedna. Maleia commanded the two whales to pull their ships alongside the anchored ships to form a larger presence, so that all four whale ships were in a row and easier to defend.

"Everyone out of the water."

"Pull the fish to shore."

"Everyone out of the water."

The minds of humans and whales quieted down as they watched for signs of a shark attack.

"Everyone out of the water."

Kilmarii The Wayfinder

"Pull the fish to shore."
"Everyone out of the water."

Maleia used her power to calm the herring, making it possible for the small vessels to pull the net to the shallow waters.

"Pull the fish to shore."
"Everyone out of the water."
"Pull the fish to shore."
"Everyone out of the water."

Finally, it was done.

Maleia sent a message out to Ouray, who was known to read humans from great distances, "Are you ready to resume hauling the fish and water?"
Ouray used the whales as go-betweens to relay his response to Maleia, "Yes. Are the sharks gone?"

"I heard no warnings."
"I will resume," Ouray replied.
"Let it be done."

The processing of hundreds of herring would begin soon and would continue throughout the night.

Chapter Five

Power of Family

Kayko returned to his father's side and waited for the evening meeting. Tozi and Ouray, riding atop Kef, joined them at the back railing.

It was at these meetings that Jyukan missed his brother the most. Unwilling to hide any thought or emotion from one another, the other human readers touched Jyukan to comfort him and acknowledge they, too, missed Mato. They were all that remained of the human knowers, the ones who could read and receive human thoughts. It was both a secret weapon and a curse.

Tozi inquired, *Ouray, how did you manage to secure enough fresh water for a full moon cycle? The lack of rain has been hard on the rivers, and I thought it would be difficult to find underground springs.*

It wasn't easy, but Kef helped me. We found a hidden spring beneath the cliff, close to the processing camp. I am making sure to store enough for everyone.

Jyukan nodded with approval.

Kayko verbally interrupted, taking over the conversation, "I am grateful I got assigned to be Lanikai's partner today. It is a huge honor. I think I'm already better than most of the Yutkis and should become Lanikai's true partner. Yachai already wants me to be with her."

Tozi raised her finger to her mouth and returned the conversation to the mental exchange of safe silence.

Kayko, you must be careful with that kind of thinking. Humility is your shield. If you walk around believing you are better than the others, you will make yourself a target of Malka, Lanikai, and Kayloni. They don't take kindly to arrogance, and their power is not something you want turned against you.

Kayko crossed his arms, his body stiffened, as he contemplated the situation.

Malka and Kayloni, yes, but Lanikai? She would not target me. I think she would prefer me to be her new partner. She knows what I am capable of doing and my relationship with Yachai.

Ouray made an audible chuckle.

Kayko, trust me, Lanikai is mated to her partner for life. That bond is not something you can disrupt.

You will understand when you are older. For now, focus on your training, not trying to take something that is not yours.

Jyukan retorted, *I am glad my son is too young to be caught up in such matters. No, Kayko. The dynamic between Maleia and her daughters is complicated. Trust us to guide you.*

Unable to resist injecting her own observations into the conversation, Tozi added, *Speaking of partners, I saw Pare flash in your mind, Ouray.*

Immediately, Ouray snapped back, *Tozi, stay out of my mind.*

Ouray, that is impossible.

Tozi flashed a side smile at her brother. *Does this woman who works well with you here also do so in the highland settlement?*

Ouray did not respond and threw up his mind shield to block further information from being revealed to his opinionated sister.

Always entitled to the last word, Tozi added, *This makes me joyful. You need to spend more time with her. It is time for you to have children, Ouray.*

Jyukan nodded. *That is good advice.*

Most of the people gathered on the deck were waiting for Maleia to speak. She was too proud to show that she was exhausted. Tozi had been monitoring the conversation and nodded to Maleia that the clan was ready to hear her.

She began, "It was a successful fish hunt. The camp will be processing the fish throughout the night and into the morning.

Kilmarii The Wayfinder

"The sharks attracted to the hunt have left the area. Yachai and Kaiyah have returned and are nearby. We will harness them in the first light. We will set traps and harvest shellfish tomorrow. Food and water will reach us soon from the camp. Eat well and go below to rest for tomorrow."

With full bellies and exhausted bodies, the men, women, and animals slowly disappeared below deck to the common sleeping quarters.

Kayko took advantage of Maleia not being able to read human minds to communicate directly with Ouray, *Have I been assigned to a hunt tomorrow?*

Yes, you are with Lanikai.

What are we doing?

Abalone and starfish.

Kayko felt disappointed that he did not get a more important role in the hunt. He had anticipated being assigned to a net crew or at the very least assigned to guard a whale. Gathering food from the tidepools was for children.

That is not very challenging, Kayko replied.

As long as she trusts you, she already thinks you are good to work with Yachai, Ouray pointed out.

Jyukan broke through, *"Everything and everyone is important, Kayko. When Yachai is ready, you and Lanikai can secure her back to the ship."*

On the second day of the hunt, the traps caught many animals. Jyukan and Maleia ordered that all killing and processing be done on land to prevent the shark alerts. This meant that the eagles and canines were needed at the shore camp to help with predator alerts.

Kayko awoke in the morning to learn that the whales, Yachai and Kaiyah, were once again attached to their ships. A mixture of disappointment and anger stirred in his heart. He wanted to seek out his father for an explanation, but he already knew the answer. It was Maleia. He had not proven himself to her yet.

Tozi grew tired of the constant back and forth of the vessels bringing the supplies to fill the storage rooms. Her frail, veiny fingers tied the cord knots to record the contents of the storage room, filled with the odd smell of smoke, herring, pelts, dried shellfish, and seal fat.

In the same capacity as the first journey to Teotihuacan, she journeyed as Maleia's most trusted advisor. Amused that the people on board forgot she was close enough to pick up on their conversations and images being exchanged, Tozi laughed quietly to herself.

She tried to make the best of it, but she understood why her late brother, Mato, enjoyed the isolation of the mountain hunts. The remaining knowers of her family: Ouray, Jyukan, and Kayko did not seem to be as burdened by this ability.

Perhaps because they are men, they can more naturally tune out the people when it pleases them.

She laughed to herself, wishing she had such discipline. Sometimes the call for human silence was so strong she once more wished for the peace of death, but then who would be the medicine woman?

Tozi walked out on the deck and nearly slipped over the edge on the seaweed drying on the deck. *Yes,* Tozi thought, *death will come soon enough.*

Lisa Newton

Chapter Six

Kilmarii Arrives

The hunt's success filled the storage hulls, and the whales had begun feeling the extra weight.

The cries of an eagle's alert broke the peace of the first travel day since the hunt.

Through the eye of the eagle, the image of a single person on a raft with a crude sail came into focus. The small raft lay near the path of the whale ships.

Maleia directed Yachai and the other whales to adjust direction to intersect with the raft. At the same time, Jyukan started his descent down the ropes.

He read Maleia's mind message.

Can you read the person on the raft? Maleia

inquired.

Jyukan glimpsed a spear piercing the neck of a green turtle and heard a song—a Yutki song— a faint echo of a memory, then gone from the stranger's thoughts.

Already engaged in a mental conversation with Ouray and Tozi, Jyukan shared the glimpse of what he had gathered. He also decided to lie to Maleia.

"Not yet," Jyukan yelled up toward Maleia.

Kayko's mind filled with the voice of Tozi.

Say nothing. Do not share what you sense. Do not share with this new wayfinder.

Kayko had no idea what a "wayfinder" was, but he assumed he was about to find out.

Maleia felt the tension in the whales, matching her own sense of unease. She raised her hand, and the chant started. The movement on the water slowed to a stop.

She sent both eagles, desperate to get another image. Every member of the clan and animal was up on deck.

Yachai reverberated out a melodic warning song to her fellow whales.

The other whales answered by joining a sound so great it expanded its vibration through sea and air.

Before the eagles reached the stranger, they spotted and relayed the image of a massive bull shark swimming on a straight course for the whale Kaiyah and her ship.

Kaiyah felt the looming danger; her whale

instincts told her to flee and protect herself and her unborn calf. She turned sharply, causing the ship to roll on its side, as she began to flee to the east.

The large shark shifted its attention toward the closer whale; Yachai was next.

Ouray's whale took notice, and she began to swim to the west. She strained, trying to outpace the threat while dragging a full whale ship.

Sedna and Yachai sent frantic messages to the Yutkis, pleading to be set free.

The bull shark circled beneath Sedna, and a wave of panic surged through the Yutki teams. Although many wished to dive in and protect the whales, they had to wait for Maleia or Jyukan to signal.

The Yutki teams on the fleeing whale ships tried to settle Yachai and Kaiyah, but to no avail. The whales were not responding.

Maleia called to a nearby school of tuna, directing them to swim toward Sedna's ship, hoping to distract the shark.

Maleia's daughter, Kayloni, and her Yutki team had positioned themselves on the mast ropes, with steady hands, to aim their spears at the tuna. Seconds after the spears were released, two tunas were projected wildly in and out of the water, impaled with long shafts. The shark's attention shifted from Sedna to the wounded tuna, just as Maleia had hoped.

Maleia gathered all her remaining strength to influence the whales and sent image after image to

Kilmarii The Wayfinder

the whales, directing them to swim behind Yachai, to circle, to stay together.

Above the roar of panic and the tension of chaos, Tozi sent a message to the stranger.

We are sending warriors to kill the shark.

There was no response.

Chapter Seven

The Wayfinder

Kilmarii pulled herself up on her raft, and the sun beat down on her skin until she retreated under the shelter she had made out of her ceremonial cape.

Her desire for water was overpowering. She uncovered the turtle shell bowl and drank most of her remaining rainwater, gratefully savoring each drop.

She heard the call of a brown eagle circling above her—a sign of prosperity. Fear gripped her as she scanned it and saw a vision of Maleia, and then massive, ominous warships. They were far away, but the vision triggered fear inside her—she recognized her own kind. She quickly shielded her

Kilmarii The Wayfinder

mind, fearing the knowers on board were already trying to read her.

Knowing she had only one defense option, Kilmarii opened her mind to command Boaric to scatter the ships. The bull shark complied by swimming off toward the ships with increasing speed. Before he reached his destination, two whale ships divided off from the remaining two. Through Boaric's eyes and mind, Kilmarii saw everything.

Observing that these were not her people, her curiosity was piqued. She ordered Boaric to circle one of the remaining ships. She realized that they were afraid of Boaric and were unable to communicate with him.

While Boaric circled under a ship, his primal hunger diverted his focus to the tunas swimming nearby. Kilmarii felt Boaric's desire to hunt.

A projected thought message sent a frightening chill throughout Kilmarii.

We are sending warriors to kill the shark.

Horrified, she felt a deep panic at the thought of Boaric being killed. She tried to call him back from the danger, but he was too far away. Her control over him was slipping; she had lost him to his instinct to hunt.

Chapter Eight

First Battle - Maleia

Maleia's thoughts sharpened, her tone and quick pace coordinated with the irritation in her command. She turned to Malka, Lanikai, and Kayloni, who were standing close by. "Bring four dolphin harnesses."

Maleia's lead canine came instinctively to her. *Protect Tozi,* she commanded.

"Jyukan and Kayko, let's go see who this is."

She then raised her arms, looked off into the distance, and summoned two dolphins to the front of the boat. Their sleek forms cut through the ocean waves. Once they appeared, she and Jyukan dove into the water and harnessed them. Kayko dove in and grabbed the reins with his father. Maleia wrapped the harness reins around her arm and held on firmly. Under her control, the dolphins pulled

Kilmarii The Wayfinder

them swiftly away from the ship toward the distant raft.

Jyukan and Kayko were inundated with Maleia's thoughts and visions. Kayko had the ability to distract himself and not listen. He seldom did, especially around Maleia, as he wished to keep her favor, always.

The darkness of her thoughts focused on the figure on the raft, then back to the events of the shark attacks. It was impossible for anyone close to a knower to shield their thoughts from them. She spoke to them mentally, just like she did with Mato, with her mind wide open. The others sensed the anger that festered inside her, and Maleia's intensity, especially now, was overwhelming Kayko.

"First, they attack our fish, break our nets. Now they are turning on our ships, our whales. They are nothing but monsters! But why did they come after us and leave the person on the raft untouched? This is not normal behavior for sharks. How is that even possible?" She struggled to make sense of it. "Something has to be done about them before they destroy everything."

Kayko mentally spoke to his father, *Do you think the person on the raft can defend against sharks?*

If they could, they would be a powerful asset to our clan. He continued, *Such skills could be taught to the Yutkis.*

As they reached the raft, the dolphins slowed.

They stared at the empty raft, knowing this mysterious warrior would be forced to surface; they would simply wait.

Jyukan turned to face Maleia and stated sensibly, "We should consider the possibility that this warrior can fend off sharks." His voice and words carefully measured, "This could be a skill we can learn from them."

Maleia's thoughts were held within a swirl of emotions.

"What do you make of this warrior?" Maleia asked Jyukan.

He lied again, though this time Kayko took notice.

"She is both fish and animal seer," he answered.

Temporarily trapped beneath the raft, Kilmarii listened for anything that might give her an advantage. She recognized the harness designs of the dolphins. She opened her mind to read the three people who were circling her raft, but her heart was beating so strongly she couldn't hear anything else.

Kilmarii raised herself up on her raft. She grabbed her spear, which until that moment was acting as her shelter pole. The fabric dropped, her turtle shell bowl flipped over, spilling the remaining water. In one fluid motion, she pivoted, the spearhead flashing in the sun as she maintained her aim at Maleia's abdomen.

Maleia's eyes drifted over the girl's woven geometric design cape of black and red lying on the raft in a heap. Her blood quickened as she recognized its symbols. The girl stood bare, untouched by the marks of life - no shoes, no jewelry, no tattoos, no scars, not even a birthmark.

Her bald head, though no longer completely smooth, was starting to regrow hair pulled from the roots. Her breasts were not yet developed. Her skin reddened by the relentless sun was taut over muscles honed by swimming. She showed no outward signs of fear, yet Jyukan and Kayko could sense her panic and see her mind flashing back to horrific scenes that were undoubtedly related to being abandoned to the ocean, although none of it made sense to either of them.

Struggling not to alert Maleia, Kayko was curious beyond words. *Is she Yutki? How long has she been surviving alone?* Kayko asked Jyukan.

Before Jyukan could respond, Maleia spoke to the girl in Yutki, "We already know what you can do. Where did you come from?"

Kilmarii made no indication she understood what Maleia said. Neither did she address Kayko's silent mental questions. She closed her mind and was now unreadable. With all eyes on her, she lowered her spear, placed her huanuy over her head, and tied a belt made of leather cord at her waist. She secured her spear to the front of her by dropping it into her belt so that it drew close to her body from her left shoulder, between her breasts, and to her right hip. She reached down for her turtle bowl and extended it out to Kayko, who instinctively secured it in the front of his tunic.

"Do you know how to ride a dolphin?" Maleia asked her.

Kilmarii dove into the water and attached her right arm to the harness of Maleia's dolphin and grabbed the reins with both hands as her response.

As the dolphins glided through the swells, towing their passengers to the towering whale ship, Maleia observed the girl, her eyes narrowing as they traced the intricate red and black geometric design on the huanuy, her garment, which resembled a cape or poncho, that she wore so proudly.

A memory surfaced unexpectedly, flooding the minds of all present knowers.

The vision was from Maleia's childhood; she was very young and was watching a ceremony of a female elder wearing the same patterned tunic and long cape, standing before a council of seven. The Yutki words spoken by this elder seemed to shake the world awake, "I am Kaiyah." A surge of conversational whispers burst forth from those gathered on the ceremonial steps. Despite noticing the scars of battle thick and prominent across the elder's arms and legs, Maleia's small body warmed with joy in hearing the great warrior's voice again. Kaiyah raised her spear and let loose the pain she had held in her womb since her exile. She had brought her clan to the trading market.

Maleia knew she had just revealed a part of her past that she wished she had not, but there was nothing she could do. *Do not speak of this to me*, her mind spoke, *nor to others*.

Kilmarii The Wayfinder

Jyukan, sensing her irritation, glanced at her. Maleia was staring at the wayfinder girl. He said nothing aloud.

Kayko's and Jyukan's dolphins were swimming behind Maleia, and they could not see the girl's face, only her tan scalp reflecting the sun. Kayko was both impressed and intrigued. *How has she survived so long out here alone?* He had seen her swim, and she was riding the dolphin as if she had experience. *What if it is true that she can fend off sharks?* If that were true, Kayko was eager to learn from her.

He did not wish to disobey his father, but his mind betrayed him to Jyukan, and to Tozi, who was close enough to engage them. *Maybe she is a human knower?* Kayko thought. But the idea would never leave his lips. Jyukan had already lied to Maleia about that, claiming she was merely a seer. Kayko had never known his father to lie. It was also clear to him that Tozi must have also known, why else would she send out the warning to say nothing? Revealing too much now could be dangerous, for reasons even he was not sure of yet.

Jyukan's focus was on the girl, too. His mind reached out to Kayko, *Be patient, use caution. We know almost nothing about her. Don't let your curiosity get the best of you.*

Jyukan's warning kept Kayko's thoughts in check.

The dolphins were met at the side of Maleia's whale ship by Malka, Lanikai, and Kayloni, wading in the water. They were there to both welcome and take the harnesses off the dolphins. Tozi and Ouray were waiting on deck at the top of the ladder.

Maleia's mind voice broke the communication thread between Jyukan and Kayko. *She understands us. She does not speak, but she listens.* Maleia directly stated into the minds of the knowers, knowing they were always reading her thoughts. *She is not to be trusted in the water. Keep her from the whales.*

The girl, still silent in every aspect, continued to watch Maleia intently. There was no fear in her stare, no sign of submission, nor anxiety. Maleia did not like how calm this young girl appeared, as if nothing they said or did could disturb her.

As the whale ship hull neared, Kayko took in a quiet breath and sought out Yachai, the whale. *We've found a girl, Yachai,* he said, with a slight smile on his face. *This girl is a shark warrior,* he exaggerated.

Yachai's large eye shifted toward her favorite human, her ancient wisdom flowing beyond their bond. *Beware,* she warned him gently, *What you don't know can be just as dangerous as what you do know.*

I will, Kayko responded mentally, though he was imagining how he could find time to speak to the girl alone.

Maleia climbed the ladder first, leading the girl behind her. The child followed effortlessly, obediently, as though this were simply the next step in an unspoken journey.

Malka spoke what the other sisters were wondering, "Mother, who is this girl?"

Kayko followed his father up, the feeling of unease lingering around them all.

"She is the wayfinder from the raft," Maleia's tone was dismissive "She knows our Yutki language, is adept at killing fish, and apparently she can fight sharks."

Malka's face showed her surprise at learning that this small girl could fight sharks.

Kayko's mind flickered with admiration, but Jyukan interjected mentally once more with a warning, *Don't make your judgments too quickly. We don't know her true capacity yet.*

The sun hovered low over the horizon, casting a fiery glow across the open ocean. From the deck, the sky had begun to transform into a gradient of deep oranges, reds, and purples, bleeding into the soft blues of the fading day. The water surface shimmered with streaks of molten gold, setting a blaze where sky and sea met in a line that stretched endlessly westward.

Tozi and Ouray were waiting, listening intently to the mind conversation between Kayko and Jyukan; where Maleia's childhood memory still lingered. Tozi's and Ouray's eyes rested upon the girl's corded huanuy.

Why has this girl stirred up this memory? Tozi posed to Ouray. *Is there a connection between them?*

Jyukan responded, *Maleia certainly does think so. She doesn't trust the girl and makes no effort to hide it.*

The moment the girl's foot touched the deck, Tozi's expression darkened. Tozi felt she had reason to fear. She couldn't help but see the resemblance to Maleia. This girl looked as Maleia had all those years ago when Tozi found her, lost and living in the sea caves at the mouth of the great river. It was no coincidence.

Maleia saw the recognition in Tozi's eyes and knew that she would be forced to reveal more than she wished to her closest friends and family. She had not forgotten that time. She hadn't forgotten the loneliness, the secrets; secrets she thought had died with Mato, her protector.

Maleia felt a mixture of wanting to explore recovered memories and a desire to dive so deep in the ocean that no mind reader could access her thoughts. If Mato were alive, he would take her deep into the woods to hunt and regain herself, but she was so easily exposed here on the open ocean, trapped on the confines of a ship.

She dreaded the thought that she may have no choice but to bare her secrets. A flash of hate, pure hate, rose from her, and it released an internal war cry from Maleia's soul, so loud that it deafened the knowers and sent Kilmarii crumbling to her knees.

Tozi wrapped her hands lovingly around Maleia's arm and led her down to the storage room. The air in the large room was thick with the scent of salty wood planks, dried fish, and the earthy musk of pelts. The floor creaked underfoot as Tozi and Maleia entered. Piles of abalone shells gleamed softly in the light of seal-fat torches, their glow casting long shadows across the room. A large circle of worn bison and bear pelts were spread out, forming a gathering space.

On a pristine polar bear skin at the center rested an ornate helmet of hammered gold, catching the torchlight. Maleia bent over and picked it up, the weight familiar in her hands. She lowered it onto her head, the cool metal settling against her brow, and a strange calmness filled the space as the helmet's power took hold. Her mind was her own, and no one else's. The moment she donned it, the knowers' probing minds were met with silence, as the gold shielded her from them.

She took her place on the polar bear skin, her posture commanding. Jyukan descended the creaking wooden stairs behind her, carrying Ouray on his back. He placed him to the right of Maleia. Across from them, Tozi moved quietly, lowering herself onto a thick bear skin on the other side of Ouray. Her weathered hands adjusted the fabric of her robes. She then signaled to the three women in the back of the room to begin tea service. Maleia's daughters gathered in their usual places, their faces illuminated by the torchlight's dance.

Kayko followed behind his father, his heartbeat quickening. It was his first time Kayko had been allowed in this meeting, and the gravity of it pressed on him like the warm air, slightly stifling. He silently took his place next to his father, Jyukan, his hands repeatedly brushing against the smooth edge of the turtle shell he had set down in front of him.

Tozi directed the silent girl to sit on the bare floorboards behind her, her status thus made clear to all. She remained motionless, her eyes downcast, her body quiet.

The smell of fresh fish mingled with the musk of the skins, and the crackling of the torches filled the space as three Esor women moved in, wordlessly serving tea, then bowls of cooked fish to each person, including Kilmarii. The quiet clatter of bowls and the muted rustle of clothing were the only sounds until Tozi gave a nonverbal cue, and the three women ascended the ladder, leaving the room bathed in quiet and anticipation.

Above them, the faint padding of Maleia's canines could be heard guarding the vents, ensuring no ears listened from the upper deck. Maleia's mind traced back in time to the memory. She took a deep breath and exhaled slowly, her thoughts locked safely within the helmet's shielding. No one could read her mind now, not even Jyukan. The warmth of the polar bear skin beneath her secured her back safely in that moment, and as the last flickers of memory clung to her, all eyes turned to her.

Kilmarii's body was still, but her mind raced through the memories of the raft, the unforgiving sun, and the endless horizon. And, there was Kayko. The boy. She had felt his eyes on her, too, but with

Kilmarii The Wayfinder

some deeper interest. She looked up to meet the eyes of three upon her, and she realized they were knowers. She cleared her thoughts and withdrew deeply within herself.

The meeting would determine Kilmarii's fate, and the weight of it hung in the charged silence. Maleia's voice broke the stillness as she began, her control over the gathering absolute.

Maleia's voice was steady, and the weight of her words hung heavy in the air.

"We are not here for stories of the past," she said, her eyes briefly flicking toward Kilmarii before settling on each of the gathered, lingering on Tozi. "The girl can hunt in the ocean, that much we have seen. But it's not her strength or survival that concerns me."

She paused, her expression hardening.

"It's the silence that she hides behind; yet it is obvious she understands us as we speak. She knows our language, but refuses to speak. She listens, but gives nothing. I will not have a trickster among us."

Her tone lowered, more deliberate, the torchlight casting a sharp contrast on her face. "I won't let her near our people until we know what she truly is. And we will know."

Her words carried finality, her authority undisputed. The tension in the room thickened as her gaze landed squarely on Jyukan, as if daring him to oppose her. The quiet crackle of the torches was the only sound before Maleia spoke again, more coldly this time:

"Until then, she remains a stranger among us, to be watched, never trusted."

Jyukan looked over at Kilmarii sitting behind his sister, *Tozi, she is no threat. She is a child with the potential to be anything. Who is Maleia to assume she is anything else?*

Are you suggesting we take her into our family?

She and Kayko are about the same age.

Ouray, who had been mentally tallying the storage room stock and seemingly not concerned with any aspect of the meeting, spoke, "It makes sense for Jyukan to raise this wayfinder. She could potentially become Kayko's Yutki partner, based on the skills you say she has."

Maleia's head and body swiveled to face him. "What skills are you referring to exactly, Ouray?"

"She can fight sharks!" the overenthusiastic Kayko chirped.

"We suspect this may be the case," said Tozi, "but she will need to be evaluated by the Yutki trainers. This is correct?" She nodded in reference toward Malka, Lanikai, and Kayloni.

Malka's face sneered with disapproval, "Mother, do you feel she is Yutki?"

Maleia inhaled deeply and, on the exhale, "Yes. She is Yutki from another, faraway clan. She has been cast out to sea to meet her fate, and for this reason, we must watch her closely. She may have useful skills. She can start her training with Kayko."

Without hesitation, Jyukan stated, "And I will take her as my child."

Kilmarii The Wayfinder

The surprised members of the circle searched the faces of the others to find out more information, none more surprised than Kayko, who had not heard these thoughts form firmly in his father's mind.

This shocking declaration meant that Kilmarii was at that moment part of the clan. She was under the guidance and protection of the most respected elder in the clan. This brought instantaneous fury bubbling up from Maleia.

"Then you are to watch over her and learn how she came to be set on a raft in the middle of the ocean," she hissed.

Maleia's words, laced with distrust, had barely registered in the ears of Kilmarii. She had observed that this leader wanted control over everything, especially things about her past. *She fears me.*

"I will," Jyukan responded.

As the entire conversation had been conducted in Yutki, both verbally and mentally, Kilmarii was aware that she had been accepted into a new family with human knowers like herself and had also gained enemies in Maleia and her daughters. She had quickly been made part of their clan. She just needed time to decide how far she was willing to become part of their new world.

Now that all eyes were upon her, she kept her mind closed to the knowers' probing and weighed her words well. Kilmarii had learned long ago that words often betray, reveal too much. Silence, however, was a shield, a weapon, and at that point she had no allies.

Lisa Newton

Chapter Nine

Unspoken Secrets

The sound of her young voice echoed in Tozi's ears, and as Kilmarii opened her mind to the other knowers, each word was coupled with a momentary memory. The more Kilmarii spoke, the deeper she touched Tozi's heart.

"I am called Kilmarii."

Tozi stood and beckoned Kilmarii to come to her embrace. Kilmarii began to rise when...

Anxiety grew sharp, twisting itself around Maleia's throat, and she announced, "The meeting is ended."

She rose sharply from the polar bear skin rug. Beneath the helmet, her jaw clenched tight. Her cloak, a deep, stormy gray, swirled around her ankles as she walked across the wooden floorboards. On her silent march toward the ladder, each step was controlled, the force of her rage held back like a coiled spring, her fists subtly flexing at her sides, the gold helmet upon her head. She moved without a sound, her anger evident in the rigid precision of every step.

Tozi led Kilmarii into a small, dimly lit chamber at the back of the storage room. Kilmarii remained motionless as Tozi removed the red-and-black huanuy, revealing her bare skin. Tozi noticed how young this girl's body was and that her hair had been clearly pulled out by the roots. She flinched inwardly, thinking about such pain, and wondered what the reason was for this.

"You've been through a lot, haven't you?" Tozi said softly, running her fingers across the smooth seal-skin tunic she was holding to give to Kilmarii. Kilmarii didn't respond; her eyes remained fixed on the floor.

Tozi helped her into the new dress. She continued speaking, her voice gentle, almost motherly. She observed Kilmarii's hands were hardened with calluses from spearfishing.

"I know what you are," Tozi's voice had dropped to a whisper. "You're a human knower, like me. Like my family. You can hear all thoughts, sense our feelings. In this clan, very few have this skill."

Kilmarii remained silent, wary, but her

posture softened ever so slightly at Tozi's kindness. Tozi adjusted the tunic and sat beside her. She poured water into a wooden bowl and passed it to Kilmarii.

Kilmarii took the water but stayed quiet.

"I think you are blocking us from your mind." Tozi's voice was calm, inviting. "But does that mean you can't read us either while you block?"

Kilmarii's lips pressed together, her body tensed, because the blocking was taxing. She knew she was exhausted and afraid, and would not be able to keep her thoughts silent indefinitely.

Tozi sighed, understanding her fear. "You are part of this family now," she said, her tone warm. "We'll protect you. You don't have to be afraid anymore."

Still, Kilmarii held strong to the mental walls she had built around herself. She glanced up, her voice barely a whisper, "Who else can... do this? In your clan?"

"I can. My brothers, Ouray and Jyukan. And Jyukan's son, Kayko. We are all true knowers."

Kilmarii's eyes darted away again, her mental barriers remaining firmly in place. *Obviously, none are true Oltec,* she thought to herself, *otherwise they would simply review my memories.* She assumed they could only hear the thoughts she wished to

Lisa Newton

send them. *This is a relief.*

Tozi closed her eyes and took a deep breath in once more, sensing that the girl wasn't ready. "It's alright," she said softly. "You have been through enough. It is time we get some rest."

Tozi prepared a bedroll for Kilmarii, spreading out soft pelts beside her own sleeping place. She showed her the bowl with a lid for waste, offering practical guidance with the same calm kindness. "Don't go above deck, and definitely not into the ocean without me or Jyukan. It's not safe yet."

Kilmarii nodded, the warning strangely comforting. She felt a slight thread of trust forming between her and the elder. Despite that fact that Tozi had taken her huanuy and cords, and her turtle shell bowl and spear were missing.

Tozi reached out to Jyukan, Kayko, and Ouray with her mind. *She's blocking me,* Tozi mentally informed them. *We will need to be patient with her. She's afraid, and she doesn't know our ways yet.*

A quiet hum of acknowledgment echoed back. *She will stay with me tonight,* Tozi added. *In the morning, you and Kayko can take her, Jyukan.*

Tozi tried to sleep, but her mind was a storm of thoughts.

Kilmarii lay still, her eyes grew heavier by the minute. She fought to stay awake, blinking slowly. Her eyelids were heavy with exhaustion, yet her racing thoughts wouldn't allow sleep to overcome her. But soon enough, her body betrayed her determination, the weight of fatigue was too strong, and despite her struggle, sleep enveloped her.

Tozi watched Kilmarii's breathing develop a steady rhythm. *It's time,* she thought, calling silently for Jyukan. He descended the ladder and sat beside his sister.

The torch flame flickered softly from the center of the meeting circle, casting flickering shadows across the room. They sat close, sipping from carved wooden bowls filled with steaming hibiscus tea. The air carried the floral scent of the tea, as their minds were focused on Kilmarii, who slept soundly nearby, her chest rising and falling in gentle rhythm.

Tozi's face softened in the fire's glow, her eyes filled with quiet sadness as she watched the sleeping girl. Jyukan sat beside her, his hands wrapped around the bowl, his mind opened to the dreamscape flowing from Kilmarii. Their mental connection developed softly between them, exchanging thoughts without words as they watched the girl's mind unravel in her sleep.

She doesn't know, does she? Tozi's thought reached Jyukan, warm but laced with concern. *She has no idea that her shield drops like this.*

No, Jyukan replied, his mind calm and measured. *But we knew this would happen. It's how we'll learn her truth. And we will determine what we will share with Maleia?*

Yes, of course. She is ours now.

As Kilmarii's mental shield fell away, her dreams flowed easily into Tozi and Jyukan's shared awareness. The first dream was one of joy, where

Lisa Newton

Kilmarii leaped into the warm ocean, laughing with children her age as they used the back of a whale as a platform. Tozi felt the deep bond Kilmarii had with the whale, and a smile came to her lips as she experienced the girl's memories of a carefree childhood.

Kilmarii rolled over, her face marked with a brief moment of distress. The dream shifted, pulling Tozi and Jyukan deeper into her mind. Kilmarii was swimming beneath the ocean, gripping the dorsal fin of a small shark, her spear ready in her hand. The shark, Atok, glided smoothly beneath her, its sleek form moving effortlessly through the water.

The dream changed into a more vivid, happier feeling. Tozi and Jyukan witnessed the shark send an image, a memory directly to Kilmarii, of her younger self, standing by a tidal pool, her small hands gently cradling Atok.

She carefully lifted him from the pool, his smooth skin slippery through her fingers, and carried him to the edge of the ocean. She released him into the shallow waves and watched gleefully as he disappeared into the vast ocean.

The memory was tinged with warmth and tenderness; the bond forged between Kilmarii and Atok in that simple act was wholly unfamiliar to Tozi and Jyukan.

Kilmarii, even in her dream, recognized the shared memory. A wave of affection swelled in her heart as she mentally acknowledged the shark's message. *I remember, Atok.* Her memory added

Kilmarii The Wayfinder

details of the rocky shoreline and steep cliffs that she had once climbed.

Tozi and Jyukan felt the strength of that bond and exchanged a questioning look, both amazed by the depth of Kilmarii's connection to the shark.

She raised it, Jyukan thought, his mental tone filled with awe. *No one in our clan has ever bonded this way with a shark.*

Tozi nodded silently, her mind still processing the intimacy of the memory. *It's more than a bond. It's a partnership. They were hunting together.*

The brief glimpse into Kilmarii's mind lingered between Tozi and Jyukan.

Tozi's lips curled into a faint smile, *She was happy once,* she thought softly, her heart aching at the thought. *Look at her swimming so freely.*

Jyukan raised an eyebrow, intrigued. *She controls it,* Jyukan thought aloud, awe seeped into his mental tone. *I've never seen anything like this. Not even Maleia can reach sharks.*

The girl's mind radiated warmth and connection for that evil creature. She was speaking to it, thanking it for the hunt. Tozi's astonishment was clear.

Jyukan nodded thoughtfully. *It's clear she has the training and gifts of a Yutki. That bond with the whale was also like we have. It's deeply familial.* He paused, considering the next thought carefully. *But why was she alone on that raft? What happened to that life?*

Kilmarii broke out into a sweat, her dream

pulled her down into a nightmare, and the shared memory from her childhood faded away like mist. The warmth of Atok's memory was replaced by fear as she shared the day she was taken from the raft. Her dreamscape darkened, her breath became ragged, and a wave of dread washed over both Tozi and Jyukan. Kilmarii stirred, her body tensed as her mind plunged into a panic state. In her mind, they witnessed not a rescue, but a capture by an enemy. Fear pulsed in every heartbeat from Kilmarii, flooding the mental space shared by Tozi and Jyukan.

Tozi's hands trembled, her bowl of tea forgotten as it clattered onto the rug. Her breath caught, and before she could stop them, tears spilled down her cheeks, her heart breaking at the raw terror radiating from Kilmarii. Jyukan reached out to touch his sister reassuringly.

She's waking, Tozi warned gently.

She's more than we thought, Jyukan added, his mental voice filled with admiration. *So much more.*

Kilmarii jerked awake, her eyes wide with fear, scanning the room until they settled on Tozi, who had her face buried in her hands. Tozi, unable to raise her head, quietly wept, her body shaking with silent sobs, overwhelmed by Kilmarii's nightmare.

Jyukan reached out with his mind, his voice gentle and full of respect.

Kilmarii, shark keeper, Jyukan chose his words carefully, *your shield is down when you sleep. We have learned much about you tonight. My sister and*

Kilmarii The Wayfinder

I... he paused, hearing Tozi's thoughts intertwined with his own, *we admire your strength. Your skills. We understand more of your journey.*

Kilmarii stared, her mind reeling. The warmth of their admiration was too much, too soon, too fast to trust. The defense of her mental privacy had been so important to her, and she immediately felt flushed with being caught.

You are safe, Jyukan added, his voice more tender now. *We open our hearts and minds to you. You are part of us now.*

Tozi lifted her tear-streaked face and, through her own mental link, echoed, *You are one of us, Kilmarii. You are not alone.*

But the words were just words. Kilmarii's body began to grow cold as fear tightened around her chest. Tears streamed silently down her cheeks as she curled into herself, pulling her knees to her chest. The mental shield snapped back up, closing her off from them entirely. She trembled, overwhelmed by the sudden intimacy of their understanding.

Jyukan and Tozi sat in silence, their hearts heavy with the weight of Kilmarii's pain. *She will need time,* Jyukan said softly, his eyes never leaving the small, shaking form. Tozi wiped her face, her heart aching, knowing they'd only just scratched the surface of Kilmarii's hidden wounds.

"We will give her time," Tozi whispered back aloud, so Kilmarii could hear her. Her voice was a soft promise in the trauma aftermath. "We will be here when she is ready."

And together, Tozi and Jyukan sat in the torchlight, watching over the wayfinder child who was once alone on the ocean, now bound to them in ways neither yet understood.

Over the next few hours, Kilmarii sat huddled in the dim, shadowed chamber, her eyes heavy with fatigue, but she refused to surrender to sleep. The torchlights along the curved walls had long since burned out, leaving only the faintest glows in the abalone shells.

Above her, the ceiling vents let in thin streams of cool air, stirring the stale atmosphere but doing little to ease the weight of exhaustion pressing down on her.

Chapter Ten

Family Bonds

From the small porthole, Kilmarii watched the first threads of sunlight break through.

The ship creaked and groaned, its slow movement adding to the stillness around her, amplifying the quiet moments between her shallow breaths.

She watched as Jyukan and his son, Kayko, descended the ladder with practiced ease, their silent approach putting her on edge.

She's still shielding herself, Jyukan sent to Kayko. His mental voice carried a mix of patience and concern.

I can feel it too, Kayko replied, his eyes locking onto Kilmarii, who stood still, watching them warily. He noticed she was wearing clan clothing.

He looked around for her huanuy and found it had been used by Kilmarii in her bedroll.

Kilmarii stood silently as Jyukan and Kayko approached her, exhaustion still pressing down on her body and mind. A feeling she hadn't allowed herself to feel sprang forward and caught her by surprise. As she watched Jyukan's steady gait, the way he held his shoulders back, and stood with his arms folded. He reminded her of her father, and deep ache of missing him returned.

Her father, the sole member of her family who had fought so fiercely for her to stay when others wanted her gone. The memory pulled at her, vivid and painful. She recalled how, in the end, even he had to accept what was to come. He had been the one to prepare her for the exile, though she had sensed the grief behind his actions. On the day her raft was lowered into the ocean, his face was a mask of pride, hiding the deep sorrow she knew he felt.

When they cast her out into the waves, her scalp was still bloodied, stinging from where they had ripped her hair out by the roots. As she dove into the cold, salty seawater bit at her wounds painfully. Climbing up onto the raft, her arms trembling, she had seen all the people on the ship with their backs turned to her. She was no longer one of them.

Kilmarii remembered she had felt a mix of despair and defiance. She was meant to die out there on the open sea, or perhaps, to find her own way and start her own clan. Like the bees, she had been an extra female, cast out to survive or fail. She knew

Kilmarii The Wayfinder

she wasn't meant to return. Yet, she also knew in her heart that she wasn't meant to fade away.

Kilmarii moved herself back into the present.

Kayko stepped forward, holding a piece of woven cloth in his hands. It was simple, yet thoughtfully made of soft white and grey fibers, which Kilmarii did not recognize. He offered it to her, his voice gentle as he spoke, "This will help protect you from the sun until your hair grows back."

Kilmarii smiled, graciously accepting it, her fingers brushing against the cloth. She tied it around her bare scalp, nodding slightly in thanks, though she said nothing.

She, however, did notice that Kayko had an easy smile. He looked at her with something close to admiration, though she couldn't fully understand why. Kayko was different from the others. There was a playfulness that she hadn't seen in the others of this clan. If it were true that she was part of this family, then Kayko was her brother. She liked the idea that these human knowers could only hear the words she chose to project to them. In her own knower clan, many could read through the memories of others at will. Her mother could. If she had been chosen at the ceremony, then she would have been trained to take over her mother's priestess role.

Unknown to her, Kayko was feeling the same joy of having a sibling like himself. He wanted to bond with her. His curiosity about her grew with every passing moment. He wondered what it meant to be a shark knower, something his father had mentioned in quiet admiration. Kayko wanted to ask her, *How do you speak with sharks?* He hoped one day she would teach him, and he imagined the adventures they could have together, learning from each other.

But Kilmarii kept her mind blocked and Kayko was unaware of Kilmarii's thoughts about him.

Tozi extended her hand and touched her brother, then her nephew on the shoulders. *It is better for all of us if Kilmarii keeps her mind closed. As a human knower, she will be seen as a threat by Maleia, but as a Yutki, she will be accepted. We must all agree that Kilmarii is a fish and animal knower only.*

And a shark knower! Kayko added.

No, Kayko, we must say only that she is a shark seer who hunts sharks for her protection as well as ours. Tozi raised her hands into the air, and clarified, *This we will tell Maleia we learned last night from her dreams.*

As Jyukan and Kayko guided Kilmarii down the narrow passageways of the ship, the constant creaking of the whale ship beneath her feet became a familiar rhythm. They arrived at their family quarters in the main chamber. Inside, Tozi had already prepared a bedroll for her, along with a small wooden bowl and a pair of leather-wrapped sandals; the fresh scent of the newly made shoes lingered. Kayko noticed that Kilmarii's turtle shell and spear were missing.

Kilmarii The Wayfinder

Kilmarii's chest tightened, a brief but unmistakable swell of gratitude threatening to soften the walls she'd built rose into her throat. She pushed it back down.

Kayko turned to her, his eyes bright with enthusiasm, "Would you like to explore the ship with me? I can show you how we live here and help you get familiar with everything."

Kilmarii nodded cautiously. She had learned not to trust kindness too easily, but the idea of exploring was better than staying trapped in a room with the elders trying to get into her thoughts. Kayko's energy was infectious, his mind radiating excitement. It had been a long time since she was with a child her own age.

I'll take Kilmarii on a hunting dive, Kayko suggested mentally to Jyukan. He sent a burst of eagerness, already imagining the plunge into the deep ocean.

Jyukan paused, sending a firm mental message back. *"No, not yet. Maleia hasn't given her permission to enter the water."*

Kayko's shoulders dropped slightly, but he didn't argue. He turned to Kilmarii with a forced smile, "We can't dive today, but I will show you the workings of this ship."

Kilmarii gave a small nod, the disappointment barely registered on her tired face. The ocean had always been her refuge, but here, on this whale ship, she was limited by the rule of Maleia.

Jyukan cleared his throat and stepped forward

Lisa Newton

to explain. As Jyukan spoke, delivering Maleia's orders that Kilmarii would be considered an Esor until she graduated from Yutki training, his firm words had an underlying warmth, and it struck her deeply. She felt a growing bond with him, something protective.

"Until your Yutki training begins, Maleia has assigned you to work as an Esor. You'll help prepare meals and handle waste disposal. And, Kilmarii, it is best that you speak instead of share minds until we know it is safe for you."

The image of Maleia floated into her mind suddenly, unbidden, the way it had when the eagle first sent it to her. She knew then that Maleia had been cast out, too, a survivor of the ocean just like herself. But there was a mystery in Maleia that Kilmarii couldn't quite unravel. *Why can't Maleia read minds?* she wondered.

Kayko grabbed Kilmarii's hand, a grin spreading across his face, and pulled her playfully across the ship's deck. The salt-tinged air whipped past them, and a laugh escaped her as she felt the roughness of his calloused fingers against her own. He pointed excitedly to the open-air kitchen where the Esors were busy preparing meals. The sizzling of fish on hot rocks mixed with the crashing waves, and Kilmarii caught the smoky aroma of grilled seafood.

Kayko explained how the waste pots were cleaned, the contents dumped at the back of the ship and washed out instantly with the rushing seawater.

Kilmarii The Wayfinder

He showed her the vessels being lowered from the sides of the main ships, and Kilmarii watched in fascination as Esors expertly handled the ropes.

Her eyes widened when he led her to the harness room, pointing out the intricately designed harnesses for the dolphins and whales. She reached out, running her fingers over the smooth leather, marveling at the craftsmanship.

But the best part came when they climbed the ropes of the mast. The thrill of height and the sway of the ship beneath them made Kilmarii's heart race, and for a moment, she held her breath and reveled in the happiness she felt.

Once they settled on a high perch, a steady breeze tugging at their hair, they began to talk in earnest.

"Do you hunt fish often?" Kilmarii asked, curiosity sparked in her eyes.

"All the time," Kayko replied, smiling. "I made my first spear when I was six."

"Me too," she said, her face lit up. "My father taught me."

"Same here," Kayko nodded, the mention of her father bringing a softness to his voice. "Did he show you how to hunt, how to survive out here? Did he teach you how to read sharks?"

"Read?" Kilmarii's brow furrowed. "What do you mean?"

"No one in my clan can read them," Kayko admitted, looking out at the ocean, his expression darkening. "They're feared, ever since one killed my mother."

Kilmarii's face grew grim as the weight of his words sank in. There was a moment of silence. She felt the pain in his voice, and it resonated with her own memories. Without much contemplation, Kilmarii touched the back of her hand to Kayko's cheek and opened her mind.

"But we're good at reading the stars," Kayko continued, forcing a smile. "That's how we navigate..." Kayko paused in mid-thought. He realized that she had switched to mental conversation.

My father taught me that, too, Kilmarii replied into the mind thread, smiling back. A shared understanding developed between them, a connection that felt deeper than words, as time slipped by, and the two became friends. They would have remained locked into each other's minds if Kayko had not realized that both their stomachs were growling.

Come on, Kayko said, tugging her hand again. *Let's get something to eat.*

They effortlessly descended the ropes, their bodies doing whatever their minds commanded. He led her to the back of the deck, where he asked if there was food available. Pare handed them corn cakes with smoked fish, along with small bowls of water. Kilmarii took a cautious bite.

As she chewed, she couldn't help but think, *Where do you keep the fresh water?*

Kayko grinned, enjoying her curiosity.

Kilmarii The Wayfinder

We store our water in the sides of the ship, he started to explain, but he was interrupted by a sudden commotion. Ouray had arrived, riding atop Kef. The sight of him with the massive creature beneath him stunned Kilmarii. She froze, her mouth slightly open in shock. She'd never seen anything like it. Her mind raced; the newness of the sight reached Ouray. Instantly, Ouray's eyes locked onto her. She felt an overwhelming pressure from her forehead, across the temples, and above the ears, as if someone was rifling through her memories.

No... she thought desperately, but it was too late.

Ouray's voice echoed in their heads, smooth and firm. *I am here to take you to my ship, Kilmarii, to work with me today. Kayko, you will also come.* While he spoke, her mental defenses stripped away, and she felt exposed, vulnerable.

Kayko, sensing Kilmarii's unease, intertwined his fingers tightly around hers.

It's going to be okay, his voice whispered in her mind, trying to offer comfort.

Ouray sent a mental message out, *We will be back for the meeting, and the four of us... I should now say five of us will meet in Tozi's meeting circle before sharing what we have learned about our little wayfinder.*

Chapter Eleven

A Nek Apprentice

Kilmarii climbed down the rope and wooden ladder onto Ouray's small vessel he used to transport Kef during ocean voyages.

She watched as Kef was lowered into the center of the oddly constructed vessel by a rope and pulley system attached to his harness, with Ouray remaining in the saddle. The vessel required four people to paddle them to Ouray's ship.

Kef would much prefer to swim, but I haven't found a ramp configuration that will support him and still maintain the structural integrity of my ship.

Kilmarii comprehended most of what Ouray's mind shared with her and was intrigued.

Kef can swim? she asked.

Oh, yes. He can also be below for longer than any Yutki, Ouray boasted with pride. *Back home, I*

Kilmarii The Wayfinder

reside on a lake in a high settlement, and we often swim.

Kilmarii received an image from Kef of him and Ouray swimming together. She saw Ouray swimming with a body harness that straightened his legs and bound them like a fish skeleton. In his hands, he grasped wooden dolphin-like fins, made of sea skin with some structure beneath, that latched on with a cord below his shoulder.

Kilmarii started her first conversation with the man who would change the direction of her life forever. *Ouray, what bones do you use to build your swimming harness?*

A smile spread across the usually furrowed brow of Ouray, and he sent Kilmarii the mental image of him creating it out of Adobeninae walrus bones. He was pleased the raft warrior was full of curiosity and possessed an analytical mind, not unlike his own.

Kilmarii stepped onto the wooden deck, breathing in the sharp tang of dried herbs mixing with the salt of the sea. Wanahi, the massive whale pulling the ship, reverberated a low sound through the wood beneath her feet, filling the air with an anxious resonance.

She is still on alert from the giant shark you sent to terrorize her. Ouray paused, in mid-chastisement, and then softened his tone, *Ahh, do I understand correctly that you were observing us through the shark, not attacking?*

I was doing both, she stated firmly, her brow

furrowed defensively.

Ahead of her, the entrance to Ouray's storage room came into full view, a wide ramp opening into a sprawling chamber. Ouray sat atop Kef, his giant armadillo, whose tough shell gleamed faintly in the dim light filtering down from the deck above.

She continued, *When I heard Tozi speak, and saw Maleia commanding the eagles, I thought your ships were coming to kill me.*

Kilmarii stepped inside, trailing her fingers along Ouray's medicine walls. There she found lines of carefully arranged wooden shelves stacked with a large assortment of wooden bowls and grass reed baskets filled with many varieties of dried plants.

Is it possible for you to explain more about why you were set out onto the ocean and why you fear your clan? I can't make sense of what I am seeing in your memories, said Ouray.

Kilmarii looked around hesitantly, glancing toward Ouray, *Are we far enough away from the others?*

Ouray's finger tapped his head thoughtfully, *Far enough. It's only me who hears your thoughts now*, he said calmly, the sound of his voice low and assured, *and I've already experienced your thoughts on this matter, but there are gaps. So, let us remain honest and continue speaking through our thoughts, as only we have the power to do.*

Kilmarii's hand paused, hovering over a small stone bowl of dried ginger root. Her stomach tightened, wondering just how much he knew about her past and her secrets.

Yes, Ouray answered her unspoken question, his voice carried a soft reassurance, *I am the only person who knows you can control as well as see into the minds of humans, animals, fish, and even sharks. There were three others like us: My mother, her mother, and Mato. I agree with Tozi, Jyukan, and Kayko, your mind powers are best kept secret for now. I think it's best to let them believe I am the only one who has this level of power.*

After taking in Ouray's decree, the room felt smaller, and a thick silence settled in around them. She glanced to her left, spotting her sea turtle shell and spear leaning against a corner, beside her familiar huanuy. She then saw the cords she had crafted spiraled and tucked underneath.

Maleia... she began, uncertain the name would successfully escape from her mouth.

She would see you as a threat if she knew you had power she did not. Ouray mentally interjected, filling her head with his voice, while glancing down at Kef, who had shifted his weight, his heavy shell brushing against the wall. *But she won't know, as long as she does not see in an animal's or fish's memory that you have controlled them. You can manage that, can't you? And only Tozi, Jyukan, and I know you can speak with sharks.* And in a slight chuckle, he added, *Kayko thought you hunted sharks.*

He waited to allow Kilmarii to read all that he

was thinking on the subject. He continued, *You will become valuable to our clan and to Maleia, if you can protect us from shark attacks. We will discuss this more in the meeting tonight.*

Kilmarii shifted, feeling both exposed and yet, strangely protected. The tension eased as Ouray continued, a glimmer of interest lighting his eyes, *You have something rare, Kilmarii. You could be trained by me, if you wanted. I could show you the ways of our clan: how to be a healer of the mind, the body, the spirit.* He paused, letting her absorb the offer.

The weight of his words filled the air between them. Above, hung cords crisscrossing the ceiling, leaves and flowers hanging, drying in the room's warmth. A saddle hung from a peg on the far wall. Kilmarii noticed Ouray's bedroll perched in a loft above it, where he could easily pull himself up, just above where Kef slept.

Something prickled in her mind, a question just starting to form. She tried to pull it back, but Ouray's faint smile told her he'd already caught it.

Maleia reads and can control animals, yes, and from great distances, but not human minds, he clarified. *That gift is in my blood's legacy. My brother, Mato, could read humans and animals both. My grandmother could do the same, and my great-grandmother...,* Ouray let out a slow breath, a flicker of respect in his eyes. *They could reach into others' minds deeply. They could sway animals and bend human emotions. Mato was able to control the*

Kilmarii The Wayfinder

animals of the land, animals of the sea, animals of the sky, and the thoughts and emotions of humans from a long distance. As I can too.

Kilmarii's eyes widened as her heart and mind betrayed her to Ouray. Yet, he held her in his sight, his tone reassuring and steady. They were both coming to the realization that they shared the same blood.

Ouray continued, *That power has presented differently with each generation. From a long distance, I can understand animals; I can communicate with them, but people...people I cannot sway unless I am touching them.* He glanced toward the door, where the silent nephew listened. *Kayko cannot reach as far as I can—he must be very close. My siblings, Tozi and Jyukan, have similar powers to me, over animals, but not as far-reaching as mine.* He moved his torso closer, his face serious, *They can all read the mind messages you wish to share if they are close, but they can't retrieve your memories against your will, like I can.* He paused in contemplation, *I know what you are capable of Kilmarii.*

Kef's claws clicked against the wood as he shifted, giving Kilmarii a curious look at this curious animal. She felt a faint tug of amusement in her mind—an image of herself, eyes wide, perhaps looking a bit overwhelmed. She looked at Ouray, who nodded as if confirming the message from Kef. The corners of Ouray's eyes crinkled in a small smile.

Kilmarii's worst fears were confirmed. She found herself adopted into the Oltek, the most powerful ancient clan. Yet, Ouray was the only strong one left among them.

...and if this is true, when I left myself unprotected, you read my memories?

Ouray explained, *Kilmarii, you have a choice. As you know, I have read your memories. I know your fears. I know your secrets. I also know you are frightened of the future. All this, I will keep between us in confidence, for our abilities bring with them both respect and fear amongst the clans of my people.*

Ouray watched Kilmarii digest all that he had explained. Seeing the young girl within the warrior before him, he watched her twist the cloth of her hair scarf as if by habit. In some ways, she was as ancient as he felt, and in reality, she was a child who had already experienced a lifetime. And the hope and joy he felt in finding another like himself, a child gifted to him by the ocean, was contained behind his shield from her.

He continued, *I can take you as my apprentice, and we will train you to take our places among the Neks and Esors when the time comes.*

Who are we? Kilmarii inquired.

Tozi will become your clan mother, Jyukan will be your father, Kayko will be your brother, and I will be your most loyal friend and uncle. You are already one of us; now all you need to do is start acting like one of us.

Kilmarii The Wayfinder

Ouray's words drew her back into her body. Kilmarii lowered her eyes, processing it all, her heart racing. There was no sense in trying to keep her thoughts shielded from Ouray; after all, having him around was like being back home in the temple, living amongst her own family members once more. Only, this time, she was being offered training, protection, and a family that saw her as an asset. Even at her young age, she knew this was the work of the great Mother Earth and the great Father Sun.

Ouray smiled broadly, tilted his head, opened his arms wide, and turned his palms up. *How well can you read beyond my projected thoughts, Kilmarii?*

The invitation to read Ouray's memories made Kilmarii's heart race. It had always been forbidden for her to do so. She had never attempted it. Panic tightened around her, and she couldn't breathe.

Calm yourself, Ouray spoke meditatively into her mind, *I will show you how this is done another time. For today, I will have you and Kayko assist me in making pain medicine for Tozi.*

Ouray and Kayko exchanged a long look. The exchange of thoughts was done in a language Kilmarii did not understand. Kayko's demeanor brightened, and he walked over to stand next to Kilmarii.

A wretched smell filled the room with an instant acknowledgment that Kef had defecated into an open trough, of which Kilmarii had not noticed prior. Four people entered; two wrapped and carried away the dung, and the others flushed the trough with ocean water. The water flowed at an angle along the bottom of the trough and into a collection bladder. They removed the bladder and dragged it up the ramp.

Kilmarii thought this was clever.

But first, let's clear the air, Ouray gestured for Kef to approach the shelves on the left. Kef stepped forward, his claws scraping lightly against the stone floor. Reaching up, Ouray grasped a braided leather cord connected to the shutter mechanism. With a firm pull, the cord slid smoothly through a polished stone ring embedded in the dark wood joist above. The shutters creaked open, letting a fresh breeze flow through the room, stirring the air.

For the rest of the day, Ouray and Kilmarii worked in careful tandem, preparing pain remedies with grinding stones, smooth wooden bowls, and fresh water brought on board after the hunt and stored deep in the ship's walls. They started by crafting a sweet tasting tea made with licorice root (glycyrrhiza glabra) and anise hyssop (agastache foeniculum), a tall, purple-flowered plant with fragrant leaves that carried the flavor of mint.

The scent will bring them comfort before the medicine even starts to work, Kilmarii absentmindedly shared out, inhaling the fresh aroma as she broke the brittle leaves into her bowl.

Ouray had harvested many of his plants from the wide, open lands east of the settlement highlands, carefully drying the plant's pale green

Kilmarii The Wayfinder

leaves and lavender blooms for this purpose. Together, they ground the dried roots, leaves, and flowers, releasing their herbal essence, and mixed them into melted beeswax to create a smooth paste to ease the pain of aching hands, shoulders, and knees of Tozi and others in need.

"You should fill an abalone shell for yourself. It will ease your sore body and help you sleep tonight."

Hearing his audible voice suddenly felt strange to Kilmarii. She stacked the filled abalone shells into Ouray's saddle bag. Ouray reached down and opened his hand. In his palm were two large gold earrings that looked like rolled tree bark, encircling each ear.

These are for Maleia.

Kilmarii knew instantly what the earrings were and what they were for; to prevent human knowers from entering their wearer's mind.

Once we are back on her ship, I will deliver them to her. Maleia does not want the others to know her past. If she knew you could read her, you would be in great danger.

And you are going to teach me how to read and control my enemy?

Kayko broke his silence to answer her question. *Maleia is not my enemy, and she does not have to be yours.*

The day ended, Ouray, Kayko, and Kilmarii stepped aboard Maleia's ship, their movements in sync, as their minds were now detectable by the other knowers. The ship slowed beneath their feet. The volume of the chant and the vibration from the whales' calls intensified inside the chamber. They descended into Tozi's meeting room, leaving the armadillo in the care of Pare above deck. Flickering torches cast shadows on the walls, their warm light dancing over the bear-skin rugs spread across the floor. Jyukan and Kayko lowered Ouray onto his rug.

Inside, Tozi was already seated, her face calm but her eyes betrayed the weight of the discussion ahead. The room was heavy with words yet to be spoken. The empty white bear-skin rug, reserved for Maleia, sat conspicuously unoccupied in the circle. It was a silent reminder of the secrecy of their meeting and the delicate line they would tread.

Kilmarii took a seat, her narrow shoulders casting long shadows. Her thin frame moved with a blend of nervousness and grace. Her dark eyes flickered on each person in turn, keenly aware of the gravity of the moment.

"We must decide how best to protect Kilmarii," Tozi began, her voice measured and low. Her weathered hands rested calmly in her lap, "Maleia cannot know the full extent of her abilities."

Conversation then turned inward to mind messages.

Tozi fidgeted slightly, the beads woven into her hair clicking softly. *Then what will we tell her? She's waiting for us to answer her questions.*

Ouray exchanged a glance with Jyukan, whose

Kilmarii The Wayfinder

stern expression deepened. He folded his arms, his muscled frame rigid with thought.

We tell her Kilmarii is a knower, Jyukan said, his emotions revealing his contemplation. *A knower of all creatures—in the sea, on land, and in the sky. That will be enough to explain her abilities.*

Kilmarii sat quietly, and the faintest smile rose on her lips. The knowledge that others could only read the thoughts she chose to project, which allowed her to keep most of the knowers from her innermost thoughts, was a source of comfort. She was sure they had no inkling of Ouray's offer to teach her how to delve deeper into human minds and even control them. That secret remained locked away, as secure as the unreadable walls of Ouray's own mind. She glanced up at Ouray, who had narrowed his eyes in her direction.

Ouray shifted slightly, then stated, *Maleia will need these. With these, her thoughts will be her own again. She can remove the gold helmet.*

He reached into his satchel and produced a pair of large, gleaming gold earring cuffs. They caught the light, their polished surfaces reflecting the hammering marks.

An audible murmur of approval rippled through the group.

Kayko leaned forward, his brown eyes sparkling with curiosity, *And the helmet? What happens to it?*

The helmet returns to the center of the meeting circle, Tozi replied. *After all, it was created by Mato for when Maleia needed it. Maleia's thoughts will be shielded by these earrings, as it should be that she has the privacy of thought.*

Kilmarii wondered if the helmet or earrings would work for her as they did for Maleia.

Tozi relaxed slightly, though her mind raced, gathering the thoughts from the group. She looked directly at Kilmarii, her expression softening, *Kilmarii, if you join our family, it will mean I become your mother, and Jyukan your father. You will grow as Kayko's sister. Do you accept?*

The breathing in the room fell silent, as all eyes turned to Kilmarii.

Her fingers tightened slightly on the edge of the rug beneath her. She looked at each face—Tozi's calm strength, Jyukan's unyielding resolve, Kayko's eager hope, and finally, Ouray's guarded expression.

"I accept," Kilmarii said, her voice carrying the warmth that now filled her heart.

Kayko grinned, his relief palpable. Tozi reached for a steaming pot and poured lemongrass tea into carved wooden cups, passing them around. The herbal aroma mingled with the scent of salt from the sea. As each person took their cup, Tozi produced small abalone shells filled with a fragrant, shimmering salve.

"A gift," Tozi said, her tone ceremonial. "For healing and protection. Kilmarii has prepared this today as part of this clan, and she will now be part of its care, working alongside Ouray."

Kilmarii The Wayfinder

The group drank the warm tea, which soothed their nerves, and they exchanged murmured thanks for the salve. Kayko, ever curious, spoke again, his voice breaking the brief silence. "Why do we still call the clan Yutki and Esor separately? It's confusing for everyone. Why not just one name?"

Jyukan's brow furrowed, and he answered with measured patience, by projection to bring such discourse into the safety of the silence. *The Esors are Yutkis, and the Yutkis are Esors. We are two halves of the same whole.*

Ouray jerked his head slightly; his dark eyes flashed. *Kayko has a point. Two names create two identities. It causes division.*

The atmosphere of the room tensed at his words. Jyukan's jaw tightened harder, and Tozi's usually serene expression clouded over. Kayko looked between them, his lips parting as if to speak, but the tension silenced him.

Instantly, the anger within was released. Jyukan growled, "Not here. Not now." His voice carried finality.

The meeting concluded in solemn silence. They rose and made their way to the deck. The sun dipped toward the horizon, casting a golden glow over the gathering. Maleia awaited them, her imposing figure framed by the backdrop of the endless sea. The gold earrings glinted in Ouray's hand, and he steeled himself for what was to come.

In small groups, Yutkis emerged from the sea, their skin shimmering with saltwater dripping onto the wooden deck. Most swam from their home ships, climbing up rope ladders and fishnets with practiced ease. One by one, they hauled themselves over the side, their laughter and warm greetings mingling with the creak of the ship. They made their way to the front of the vessel, where the nightly meeting, led by Maleia, was about to begin.

Among the arrivals were the clan representatives from each ship. They separated themselves from their Yutki clan members, gathering in a quiet cluster off to the side. This division caught Kilmarii's eye, and an uneasy pang stirred in her chest. Memories surfaced of her own separation, locked away within the temple grounds where she grew up. Her longing to leave those grounds and join the other children sharpened, leaving a tightness in her ribs.

She noticed Kayko was standing beside her, and felt a rush of gratitude. Kayko, now her adopted brother, was her anchor to the hope for companionship she had always wanted. She daydreamed of their future adventures: swimming through the glistening ocean waves, leaping from jagged rocks into crystal-clear pools, and yesterday's shared laughter high in the ship's mast nets. The images flooded in her mind, vivid and comforting.

Kayko sensed her emotional thoughts and stepped closer to get a better read. He liked what she envisioned. Without a word, he took her hand, his fingers warm and reassuring against her own. The other knowers, catching the silent exchange, shared subtle signs of approval. The bond between the two young ones was growing, and it softened the tension between them.

Maleia stood at the center of the gathering. Her muscular frame and long, gray hair gleamed in the setting sun. She accepted the pair of golden earrings from Ouray and handed over her helmet to him. As Maleia put on the earrings, her thoughts vanished, as her mind was now shielded from any knower's reach. Ouray, meanwhile, blocked his own mind, a skill only he had fully mastered.

Kilmarii grasped fragments of Ouray's private conversation with Maleia. Her pulse quickened, and she clenched Kayko's hand tighter. She dared not betray her awareness as Ouray's head turned sharply in her direction. He revealed nothing to Maleia, allowing her to assume many things.

Ouray signaled Kayko and Jyukan, who lifted him with ease and carried him back to where the others had gathered. The meeting began in earnest as Maleia waited for the crowd to settle. Her voice was steady and commanding; it filled the air as she scanned the thoughts of the whales tethered to the ship.

"We are on course to reach warm waters by late tomorrow night," Maleia announced, her tone as resolute as the sea breeze. "Once there, Ouray and his scouts will locate a freshwater island. The ships will anchor together, the whales will be released, and we will make camp. We will remain there for six moon cycles to train, rest, and trade at Teotihuacan."

Kilmarii listened intently, her mind swirling with the thoughts of those around her. Fragments of conversation from Jyukan, Tozi, Kayko, and Ouray wove through her consciousness, an overwhelming tide of voices and intentions. Her legs wobbled with exhaustion; her body swayed as sleep threatened to claim her.

"Kilmarii," Maleia's voice cut through the haze, sharp and clear. Kilmarii blinked herself alert as all eyes turned toward her. Maleia introduced Kilmarii by name to the gathered clan, stating that the girl belonged to another clan and possessed the abilities of both Yutkis and Esors.

Maleia explained that Jyukan had adopted Kilmarii and would raise her with the help of his siblings, Tozi and Ouray. "She will be trained in our ways and will join in the training of the new Yutki," Maleia stated with authority. After a long pause, she continued, her voice calm but heavy with significance, "It has been discovered that Kilmarii can read sharks. This is a skill no one else has. She will therefore also train under Ouray, who also holds unique gifts with animals."

These words caused a murmur in the crowd. And from them, their thoughts and questions reached the mind of Kilmarii. She realized she would need to learn the Esor language too.

Kilmarii stiffened at the mention of Ouray's abilities. She realized the full extent of his powers had not been shared with Maleia. Her chest tightened as she processed this secret, a weight she would carry quietly.

The meeting concluded, and the clans dispersed to their ships for the evening meal. Kilmarii, now too tired to eat, curled up between Jyukan and Kayko in the great room below deck. The multitude of voices faded as her eyes grew heavy.

Jyukan looked down at her, a tenderness revealed on his face. He began weaving a bedtime story on the silent thread that connected to Kilmarii and Kayko, his thoughts rich with details of Mato and Maleia's tale. In the next room, Ouray and Tozi listened quietly, the story's warmth seeping into their recollection of the past few days' events.

Kilmarii drifted off, the vivid tale filled her dreams as the rocking of the ship cradled her in its gentle rhythm.

When Kilmarii woke, her mind released the faint memories of the previous night's dream. Her eyes fluttered open, taking in the dim light of the common room. It was empty except for Kayko, who sat against the wall, arms crossed, scowling at her with thinly veiled impatience.

"We're the last ones up," he snapped, his tone cutting through the haze of her grogginess. "Now we have to clean the pots. Never be the last one up, Kilmarii. Never!"

The sharpness of his words fell on deaf ears, as Kilmarii felt more like herself today, and only nodded, her natural inclination to be the judge of the situation herself returning to her. She spotted her headscarf on the floor beside her and swiftly tied it around her head, the motion grounding her into the reality that she willed herself to stay mentally present in. Together, she and Kayko hauled the heavy pots, one by one, to the dumping area at the end of the ship.

The air smelled of salt and perspiration, the tang of the ocean mixing with the furious pace of people preparing to anchor the whaleships. As the waves crashed below, Kayko and Kilmarii dipped the pots into the salty water, scrubbing them clean with the force of the wake. The cool sea spray dotted Kilmarii's face as she worked.

Curiosity bubbled up within her, and she initiated the morning's mind-speak. *Why are these pots made of stone?* she asked. *They're so heavy.*

Memories of her previous life at the temple flickered in her mind. This granted a window for Kayko to see her past. She recalled the wooden shoots that opened through the floor, flushing waste out to the stream that ran under the temple housing, and the small, carefully constructed outhouses on the temple grounds.

Kayko sent back an immediate reply, his mental voice matter-of-fact, *The pots are made of stone, so they won't tip over in rough seas. It's better than dealing with a mess on the common deck.*

He gestured for her to follow and led her to a wooden enclosure with rows of holes cut into the floor. The salty breeze drifted through the slanted walls, and below, the endless ocean churned.

This is the ship temple where we go. His mental tone was laced with faint amusement.

Kilmarii stifled a laugh.

Without incident, they finished their task, the pots scrubbed clean, and returned to the common room. Just as they placed the last pot down, Tozi appeared at the doorway.

"Come with me," she said in a voice warmed with a blend of authority and care. "I understand you want to learn the Esor language, Kilmarii. Kayko and I will help you with that this morning. Afterward, Ouray asked for both of you to join him on his ship for lessons."

Excitement sparked in Kilmarii's chest. The thought of spending the day together, learning and exploring, brought an instant smile to her face. Kayko, too, seemed eager; his earlier irritation melted away.

In the meeting room, Tozi had arranged three bearskins in a triangle with a dark blue stone that reflected with veins of gold in the filtered sunlight. The air was heavy with the scent of burnt sage, and the room felt alive with quiet energy.

Tozi removed her cape, and Kilmarii's breath escaped her. There around Tozi's neck hung a ceremonial black jaguar necklace; its distinctive beads boasted of the significance of high-ranking. Recognition flashed in Kilmarii's eyes, and her pulse quickened.

This necklace was given to me by my

grandmother when I became the clan's medicine woman, Tozi explained, her mental voice weighted with pride. Her soft eyes landed on Kilmarii. *You recognize it, don't you?*

"Yes," Kilmarii answered aloud, her voice barely above a whisper. Her mind flooded with memories of similar necklaces worn by the temple priestesses. To have a claim to one is a symbol of power, wisdom, and a sacred connection to the spirits.

Tozi nodded, satisfied. She lifted a shallow bowl of water and passed it between them, taking the first sip herself. "Hold hands," she instructed, extending her own to each child.

The three completed the circle, their hands linking. Tozi's palm was rough and cool to the touch, a steady anchor. Kayko's grip was firm, his excitement was tangibly felt in Kilmarii's.

"To learn the Esor language," Tozi's voice spoke rich with intention, "we must first align ourselves. We will chant and sway until our minds sync, and then Kayko and I will guide the language into your mind. It is your task, Kilmarii, to practice it with Kayko until it stays."

The chant started low, a soft hum resonating from Tozi's throat. Kayko joined in. Kilmarii hesitated, her heart thudding in time with the rhythm. Slowly, she added her voice, the sound shaky at first but growing steadier with each passing moment. An energy field started to build in the air around them.

Kilmarii The Wayfinder

Their bodies swayed in unison, the movement fluid like the waves reaching a shore. The blue stone at the center of their circle seemed to pulse faintly, its surface catching and reflecting the cadence of their voices.

The energy in the room continued to build, a warm and soothing current that Kilmarii felt in her chest, her fingertips, her very bones. As their voices harmonized, she sensed the connection deepen, their thoughts intertwining. A quiet determination filled her, readying her for what would come next.

The chant transformed, the sound began reverberating off the center stone and deep into their minds. Kilmarii felt a warmth spreading through her chest, a connection threading through the three of them like a living cord.

Tozi's thoughts pressed gently into Kilmarii's, and the words and images came next, entire structures of the Esor language pulsed through Kilmarii's mind, demanding her attention. It felt as though a great river of knowledge was pouring into her, mesmerizing in its depth.

Next, Kayko added his own layer of understanding; his mental voice rippled through Kilmarii's consciousness, and she grasped, holding tight to the unfamiliar sounds and meanings. It was that moment that she felt the deepest desire to learn all there was to know about the Esor clan.

Tozi slowed down the chant, which signaled the end of the first phase. "Now," she said aloud, her voice steady, "we will practice together. You must speak it to hold it. Use it often, and it will remain with you."

Kilmarii nodded, her hands still trembling from the intensity of the experience. The day lay stretched ahead of her, filled with the promise of learning, adventure, and the steady support of her newfound family.

From his perch high on the mast rail, Jyukan leaned against the netting, the wind tugging at his hair. Below, Kilmarii and Kayko swam in unison, their strokes powerful and smooth as they raced toward Ouray's ship. Beside him, Maleia watched silently, her expression tight and her golden earrings catching the sunlight.

"They swim well together," Jyukan remarked, his voice warm with pride. "They've grown comfortable together quickly."

Maleia's lips pressed into a thin line. "Comfortable doesn't mean capable," she said, her tone cool. "It's too soon to know if Kilmarii has real value to the clan. Swimming is one thing. Everything else? That remains to be demonstrated by her."

Jyukan watched her, his brow furrowing slightly, "She's doing well, Maleia. Better than we could have hoped for. The whales have already accepted her, and that's no small thing."

Maleia's gaze sharpened, "Acceptance doesn't mean usefulness. Trusting her with the pod is a risk. We still don't know where she came from, or if her loyalty lies with us."

Kilmarii The Wayfinder

Jyukan took a deep breath, keeping his tone steady and calm, "She's young, but she's learning fast. We have the ability to guide and shape her."

Maleia folded her arms, her eyes narrowing as she watched Kilmarii dive beneath the waves and surface with a splash of laughter., "Belonging is earned, Jyukan. She needs to show that she has something to offer, something we can't find elsewhere." She paused in reflection, "Just as I have."

"She already has," Jyukan countered gently. "The whales responded to her without hesitation. And you know as well as I do that's rare, even among us."

Maleia's jaw tightened. She watched as the children reached Ouray's ship and climbed aboard, their laughter drifting off on the breeze. "How did her swim feel to her?" she asked finally, her voice laced with skepticism. "You've been paying attention."

Jyukan smiled faintly, "She missed the feel of the water on her skin. Diving into the sea, racing against Kayko, pushing herself as hard as she could brought her joy. She didn't win, but that only made her more determined."

Maleia raised an eyebrow.

Jyukan said with quiet confidence. "She has more strength than you give her credit for."

"And the whales?" Maleia pressed "Did she speak to them?"

"She did," Jyukan replied, his smile widening.

"Yachai, Wanahi, Sedna, and Kaiyah. She introduced herself, and they responded warmly. They've accepted her."

Maleia closed her eyes briefly, reaching out with her thoughts to confirm his words. The soft hum of the whales' minds brushed against her own, filled with a sense of ease and trust. Her jaw tightened, though she said nothing for a long moment.

"That doesn't mean they'll trust her when it matters most," she said eventually.

"It means she has potential," Jyukan replied, his tone firm but kind. "And potential is worth nurturing."

"And that is what our job is, Jyukan." Maleia's gaze hardened as she shifted the topic. "Let's focus on the navigation. The Bay of Harmony is close, and the currents won't make this easy. We need to guide all four ships in carefully."

Jyukan nodded, his tone calm. "And once we're in, Ouray and the rest of the Neks will scout the island for the freshwater springs?"

"Yes," Maleia said, "the island springs are key to our campsite."

"They'll find it," Jyukan said simply. "Ouray's good at what he does." His faith in his brother's skills was unwavering.

Maleia's mouth tightened once again, but she didn't argue. Instead, her sharp eyes followed the children as they vanished onto Ouray's ship. "We'll see if she surprises me," she muttered under her

Kilmarii The Wayfinder

breath. Maleia outstretched her arms and was in obvious communication with her two eagles. One turned to Ouray's ship, and the other flew ahead of their ship as a scout.

"She already has," Jyukan said softly, his eyes steady on Kilmarii's distant form. "And I think she'll continue to, if you let her."

Maleia didn't respond, her expression unreadable. But as she turned back to the horizon, the faintest flicker of uncertainty shadowed her features. The brown eagle landed on the windowsill of Ouray's room to act as Maleia's spy.

Kilmarii noticed the air in Ouray's great room was warm and fragrant, filled with the earthy, sharp scents of dried herbs and roots wrapped in cloths, some spilling out of the bowls that had lost their order and were now haphazardly shelved. The light filtered in through the woven panels, casting shifting patterns across the space. Jek, Ouray's giant companion, moved quietly, acting as his legs while Ouray affectionately stroked his ear.

Kilmarii and Kayko stepped into the room, their damp clothes clinging to their skin, leaving a trail of seawater behind. Kilmarii's eyes immediately caught on the seal-skin map spread across the sleeping deck. Its detailed markings drew her attention like a beacon. Kayko stood at her side, his head tilted downward curiously.

Chapter Twelve

Maleia's Map

The unrolled seal skin encompassed the entirety of the table.

"That's quite a map," Kayko said, his voice low with awe. "Is it Maleia's?"

Ouray nodded.

"Indeed. Maleia made this map long ago. It charts every island and important place she—or rather, we—have discovered together. It holds the stories of our journeys and shows the locations of places only Maleia knows."

As he spoke, Kilmarii edged closer to the map, her curiosity sharpening. The seal skin was soft yet durable, its surface inked with intricate lines and

Kilmarii The Wayfinder

symbols, each detail painstakingly crafted. Her gaze swept across it, searching—hoping.

And then she saw it, her homeland. The faint marking sent a shiver down her spine; her thoughts raced with memories: the curved coastline, the cliffs rising like guardians, the springs growing into narrow rivers interlacing toward the sea.

Ouray and Kayko, attuned to her mind, exchanged a glance. Ouray's expression remained steadfast, kind. "Kilmarii," he said gently, "would you show us where your home is?"

Kilmarii hesitated, her fingers hovering well above the map. She looked at Kayko, who offered her a reassuring nod. Finally, she pointed to the symbol marking her home.

Above them, the brown eagle perched silently in the rafters. It had sharp eyes for observing the scene, noting every detail with keen precision. The image of Kilmarii's pointed finger was relayed to Maleia on the other ship, the visual transmitted with a flash of clarity. Maleia stiffened when she saw it, her teeth grinding with tension, but relief flooded her when she realized Kilmarii's home was not her own.

Back in the great room, Ouray crouched beside the map, one hand lightly tracing the routes leading from Kilmarii's homeland to the Bay of Harmony, and with the other hand he motioned for the eagle to fly away. Once it had left the windowsill, he asked her, *When did you spot Maleia's feathered spy?*

Not waiting for her to reply, *We are alone now.*

Show us where your homeland is on the map.

Kilmarii pointed to a southern location off the map, then traced her path through the air to the spot where they found her on the raft.

This connection over the ocean to your home may serve us well. Do you recognize these islands? Ouray's thoughts were gentle yet deliberate.

Kilmarii furrowed her brow. *My father told me about these islands,* she responded slowly, her mind also projecting memory pictures. For the first time, Kayko was shown a glimpse of her past.

He said some have food and fresh water, but the current took me out of the bay, and I was never able to visit them, Kilmarii explained.

Ouray nodded encouragingly. *Do you remember which ones? Look closely.*

Kilmarii leaned over the map, her fingers grazing the seal skin as she studied its markings. "This one," she said finally, pointing to a symbol.

Kayko, go up on deck and let Jyukan know that we have identified the central, eastern islands as the probable campsite. Maleia can confirm this with the eagle she sent.

Kayko hesitated before stepping away.

Ouray continued, *I understand, Kilmarii, that you are learning the Esor language. We will practice it for the rest of today. It is important for knowers, to learn many languages to trade and to better the advantage of our clan.*

Can you make others do what you want them to? Kilmarii's mental voice was cautious but

Kilmarii The Wayfinder

inquisitive.

I can influence them, but I can't make anyone do my will over their own. Ouray paused, collecting his words. *For example, I know you believe that I can read your mind and memories completely, but that is not true. I can only read the memories that are easily recalled by the person themselves. I can't see into the past of someone who has repressed or forgotten their history.*

Kayko exhaled with visible relief. *That's a relief, Uncle, to know there is at least something you can't do.*

With Kayko's return, Kilmarii straightened, her mind flitting back to her father's stories. *He told me the islands farther from the coast were safer because fewer people visited them. He said this one—* she tapped the map again—*was special because it's where water lives in the Temple of the Moon.*

Ouray smiled, the corners of his eyes crinkling, and switched to Esor. "You have a good memory. That kind of knowledge will be invaluable to us." He turned to Kayko. "And you, Kayko. What do you see?"

Kayko placed his hands on the map and studied it. "The currents around that island look strong," he said thoughtfully. "We'll have to be careful guiding the ships in. But if we anchor here,"—he pointed to a sheltered cove—"all four ships may have enough space to rest safely."

"Well said," Ouray replied, approval in his tone.

Lisa Newton

"The two of you are already thinking like wayfinders. That will serve us all well."

Jek let out a soft grunt and shifted his weight, breaking the illusion that he was merely an extension of Ouray. Kilmarii's curiosity flared, and she strengthened her mental connection with Jek, peering deeper into the creature's mind.

"He's beautiful," she said carefully in Esor, her soft voice questioning her new found words. "Does he do more than help you move?"

Ouray's smile broadened, "Jek is my companion and my strength."

Kilmarii stepped closer, running a gentle hand along Jek's sturdy shell. "I've seen his kind before, but never as a companion."

Kayko grinned. "You'll find Ouray is full of surprises."

Ouray gave Kayko a playful wink.

"And I expect you both will bring your own surprises as we continue. Now, let's determine our course and see where the rest of our daylight takes us." Ouray chuckled softly and continued to speak aloud in Esor, "First, we will start with essential Nek training, stone fires, and then we'll prepare the offering for tonight's ceremony of thanks."

Excitedly, the children exchanged a windstorm of mind messages as the room filled with anticipatory energy. Stone fire making was a skill that started with selecting the correct rocks, provided the user knew how to strike them together and grow the fire. Their desire to hone this skill was

Kilmarii The Wayfinder

high, for while all clan members were taught how to make fire, it was a new skill for each of them to master.

A strong motion was felt, and the ship tilted to one side then rolled to the other. The whales started vocalizing.

Upon entering the bay three days ago, the whales started showing signs of stress and discontent. As the ships neared the island, the whales began to act erratically. The warmer water churned with their defiant tail strikes, displaying their distress, and the clans and animals aboard the ships were tossed and thrown about.

Maleia's voice cut through the chaos. "Release the whales!"

Jyukan's deep voice commanded, "Start the stop chant!"

Together, along with the rest of the Yutkis, Maleia and Jyukan tried to calm the whales and convince them to stop to be unharnessed.

The stop chant rose from the ships in unison, voices weaving a rhythm of urgency. Slowly, the whales began to calm and drift to a stop, their immense bodies longing to be free from the tension of pulling a heavy ship.

Malka, Lanikai, and Kayloni dove to their ship's whales without hesitation.

"Release!" Malka shouted before vanishing beneath the waves.

On Ouray's ship, the scene was developing into something more frantic. An inexperienced crew scrambled, unsure how to handle the situation, as their Yutki members were all aboard Maleia's ship.

Maleia turned to Jyukan. "There's no time, contact Kayko to dive! Free Kaiyah before she injures herself or the ship!"

Kayko hesitated for a fraction of a second, then nodded sharply. "I'm going," he said, resolute.

On the opposite side of the ship, Kilmarii took a deep breath. She didn't wait for orders. Without a word, she dove into the water, her body slicing through the surface like a blade.

"What is she doing?" Maleia shouted, her voice edged with panic.

"She knows what's at stake," Jyukan interrupted, his eyes fixed on Kilmarii's descending form, "let her do it."

As Kilmarii reached Kaiyah's whale harness latching, her memories surged unbidden, spilling into Kayko and Ouray's minds. Her memory scenes of working with whale ships in her recent past displayed more than she would have liked, but she had no control in that moment.

Kayko's breath hitched, his thoughts brushed against Kilmarii's. "You've done this before," he projected mentally, astonished.

The knowledge that Kilmarii was demonstrating struck Ouray like a tide. He gripped the saddle tightly, his mind whirring. *Who is she, really?* He silently vowed to speak with her later, to uncover what else she knew, beyond what she wanted them to believe. He realized that this girl

Kilmarii The Wayfinder

had secrets that he had yet to discover.

When Kayko and Kilmarii surfaced, gasping for the ladder, the tension on deck shifted. The other knowers, now within range, heard Ouray's mental voice.

Kilmarii, he said sternly, *you defied Maleia's orders. All eyes are upon you now. You are no longer the wayfinder from the ocean who can fight sharks; you are now the one who crossed Maleia and Jyukan. You must tread carefully.*

Her heart pounded as she met Ouray's eyes.

I only wanted to help, she said mentally, her body trembling.

You did help, Ouray admitted, his tone softening slightly, *but you are drawing much attention to yourself. From now on, speak only with words. Others must think you are one of them, and not learn that you are a knower.*

Tozi's voice reached into the conversation. *He's right. From this moment on, for your safety and ours, you are no longer permitted in knower meetings.*

Kilmarii hesitated before she spoke, "What? But I—" she said in Esor.

You may stand with us at the nightly clan meetings, Ouray continued, his words firm, *but only as family. Nothing more.*

Kilmarii clenched her fists, the weight of their words heavy on her heart. Kayko stepped closer, his voice quieted. "You did the right thing," he said, touching her shoulder. "That's what matters."

With the whales freed, Kilmarii turned and faced the back of the ships. She watched in quiet awe as the Esor and Nek crew members sprang into action. The sails unfurled, catching the wind, and the ships moved gracefully toward the island's eastern side. They steered the vessels into a secure rock-enclosed cove, their coordination seamless.

On deck, the Yutki clan members worked to calm the animals, murmuring softly to frightened creatures, while others watched the whales swim away. Kilmarii watched their focused efforts, feeling a pang of discomfort. She realized she had no clear task, no direction, no purposeful activity.

Her wandering feet took her below deck, where she found Ouray's quarters in disarray; his herbs spilled across the floor, shelves toppled, and supplies scattered. Kilmarii paused, biting her lip as she surveyed the mess. She walked over and picked up her sea turtle shell, and began to clean and restore the room. She handled each herb with care, doing her best to sort and return the items to their proper places.

Meanwhile, above deck, she glimpsed Ouray at the top of the ramp. He sat tall, directing his animal companion, a powerful creature, to load and unload supplies using a pulley system. The Neks and Esors worked alongside him, preparing a campsite with practiced efficiency.

When Kilmarii finished in the room, she stepped back and exhaled, looking at her handiwork. It was not perfect, but it was better. She

Kilmarii The Wayfinder

lingered for a moment, listening to the sounds of the bustling deck above, before going back up to find her place among the clan vessel going to the main ship for the meeting.

Kilmarii spotted the knowers heading for the stairs below deck. Tozi met her eye and stated loudly, "You are not permitted in this meeting."

Jyukan and Kayko nodded in agreement and descended down the stairs. Tozi's expression was grim as she added, "You're no longer permitted in knower meetings. You may stand with us at the nightly clan meetings, but only as family. Nothing more."

These interactions were noticed by many clan members on deck.

Kilmarii felt the weight of their words settle on her shoulders like an anchor, and she responded by walking away. Before she got too far, Kayko's quiet assurance soothed the sting.

Later, as they waited for the clan gathering, Kayko shared Maleia's praise for their success during the knower meeting. The acknowledgment was unexpected, and it lifted Kilmarii's spirits, but she wished she had been present to hear it directly from Maleia's mouth.

When the clan meeting began, Maleia stepped forward. Her voice carried over the gathered crowd, steady and filled with uncharacteristic emotion. She thanked the clan for their efforts in saving the whales, the ships, and ensuring their arrival at the island. She expressed joy, relief, and humility—

feelings rare for her to share. She raised her arms high, as she called on the spirits in the sky, lowered them when she spoke of the earth, and lowered further for the waters. From the gathering, calls of affirmation rang out. The clan began to celebrate, congratulating one another and speaking cheerfully as they dispersed.

As the night settled, Tozi placed her hands on Kilmarii's shoulders. "You need to eat and rest now," she said firmly.

Kilmarii nodded and moved to the back of the deck. She walked side by side with Kayko. The weight of the clan's eyes followed her every step. She was handed a bowl of hard-boiled eggs and fresh water. Curiosity piqued, she asked the Esor girl who handed her the eggs, "Where were these gathered?"

The young woman's face lit up in surprise, "You speak Esor!" She recovered, then said warmly, "The eggs come from one of the ships. It has a birdhouse. Would you like to see it?"

Excitement bubbled within Kilmarii, and she smiled, feeling an unexpected sense of connection.

"Yes," she said without hesitation. The young woman introduced herself as Tesi, and for a moment, it felt as though Kilmarii had made a friend. But their moment was cut short when an angry-faced woman called Tesi back to the cooking fire.

Seated next to Kayko, Kilmarii peeled her eggs slowly, the interaction replayed in her mind. A

Kilmarii The Wayfinder

small smile tugged at her lips; the warmth of Tesi's kindness lingered, even amidst the uncertainty.

She and I were close friends, Kayko said.

Why are you not now? Kilmarii asked with her mouth full of delicious egg.

When we moved to the Yutki settlement, we never saw each other again.

You can see her right there, Kilmarii rolled her eyes in Tesi's direction.

She probably doesn't remember me.

You and I can both read with all certainty that she does remember you, and you know it. Kilmarii wondered how Kayko could forget so easily that they were human readers, but then she remembered he may not have been close enough to read Tesi.

The animated facial expressions being exchanged between Kilmarii and Kayko were noticed by Jyukan. His bad temper flared, and he chastised, *Always speak aloud.*

Jyukan did not just see the children recoil, but he also felt their scared emotional reaction. He felt a ping in his heart because he realized that he had stifled a moment of them bonding as siblings. His concerned self-reflection soon ended when he realized that both getting disciplined for misbehaving together was also bonding for siblings.

That evening, under the gentle sway of the anchored ships, Kilmarii and Kayko settled down next to Jyukan. The warm day had cooled fully into night, and the rhythmic lapping of waves against the hull soothed their minds. Jyukan's deep voice carried a story into the quiet: a tale of his childhood adventures in the highlands with Mato and Tozi. He wove images of danger, laughter, and the mischievous trouble they found together in their youth.

In these memories, Kilmarii recognized a few faces, but the one she was most pleased to learn was that of Mato's. Kayko had held no memory of him, as he had died before Kayko was born.

Kayko listened intently; his eyelids grew darker behind each word. Before long, the steady breathing of both children signaled they had drifted into sleep.

Jyukan fell silent, allowing himself to recall intimate moments with Kayko's mother, while silent tears of mourning rolled down his cheeks.

From his ship, Ouray rested upright in his bed, focused, making his mental rounds, checking in on the status of the clan by reading specific leaders. This was a nightly ritual. He turned his mind toward Kilmarii's resting form. As he reached out to her, he closed his eyes, letting his mind stretch outward. He had done this many times before, gently probing memories to better understand his clan and to predict their needs. Yet when he reached toward Kilmarii's thoughts, he found her barrier had returned, a shield, strong and unwavering. Ouray pushed harder, testing its strength, but the resistance remained impenetrable.

Frustration swelled within him. Only his grandmother had ever blocked him like this, but this young stranger, a girl pulled from the ocean, could do the same. His thoughts began to examine the implications. A flicker of unease threaded through his curiosity.

He stepped back, his brow furrowed and reached out mentally to his brother and sister.

She's shielding herself, he said, his tone sharp in their shared mental link. *As she sleeps, I can't see her thoughts at all.*

Tozi responded first, her mental voice calm and amused. *Is it probable that she is more powerful than our brother, Ouray? She's too young to know her full self. Do not be alarmed. I believe she closes herself off not because she can, but because it is her natural protection.*

Jyukan joined in, his thoughts a mix of surprise and skepticism. *We all have some ability to shield our thoughts. What are you saying, Ouray? Do you fear this child may be your equal?*

Ouray's gaze shifted towards the night horizon, where the moonlight glinted off the water. *I'm saying she could be as powerful as Grandmother.*

A tense silence followed, the weight of his words settling heavily between them. Tozi broke in, her voice laced with sensible caution, *If that's true, she has the potential to be even more dangerous than we thought. Ouray and I should take her with us to the highlands, away from the power of the water, and ground her in the foundation of the earth. She can train under both of us, brother.*

Our focus has to stay on the clan and the island, Jyukan added, *without a great consideration of what she is or whatever she might become—let us first get her through Yutki training. When the time comes we can continue her Nek training with Ouray and you, Tozi, in the highland. Remember, Kilmarii is not our grandmother; she is our child.*

Ouray didn't respond immediately. Instead, he let his mind linger on the shield he could not penetrate, on the words "our child", on the girl who held more secrets than anyone had seemed to realize.

Finally, he spoke, *we will watch her closely.*

His message conveyed his deep reflection, *and we should all work on strengthening our own shields to keep this information from both children. If we keep them safe, grow them strong, then the future of our clan is certain.*

Meanwhile, Kilmarii stirred in her sleep, unaware of the scrutiny she was under. Dreams flit through her mind, fragmented and fleeting—images of the ocean, the whales, and faces she barely remembered. Something in her stirred, a faint unease that pulled her from the depths of her slumber. But when she opened her eyes, the sight of Kayko sleeping soundly next to her and Jyukan's steady breathing calmed her once more. She rolled onto her side and placed her hand on Kayko's shoulder.

Chapter Thirteen

Yutki Lessons

Golden morning light had not made its appearance in the common room, and in a dark corner, Kayko rolled a small shell between his fingers, his movements brimming with youthful energy.

Kilmarii opened her eyes slowly, looking through her eyelashes to find Kayko's feet. She adjusted her headscarf, her eyes shimmering with anticipation for the day ahead.

"We are not the last ones today!" Kayko whispered in Esor, his voice cutting delicately through the silence of the room. "No chamber pots for us. Someone else gets the fun of that job!"

Kilmarii whispered back, also speaking in Esor. "It is the first day of Yutki!"

Kayko leaned closer, his voice dropped as if he

was about to reveal something precious, "Yutki school is incredible. Maleia's daughters run it, and they are amazing. You will see."

Maleia's daughters? Kilmarii repeated mentally, her curiosity sparking.

Kayko's grin widened, the shell momentarily forgotten as he eagerly explained. "Malka is the oldest. She is like her mother, Maleia. She is strong, commanding, and always in charge. She organizes everything and teaches us how to drive fish into the nets and how to speak the Yutki language, which is easy for the two of us."

"Then there is Lanikai. She is my favorite cousin." His voice dropped conspiratorially. "Do not tell the others. She is patient and kind, and she reminds me of Tozi. Lanikai used to take me hunting with her in the highlands."

Kilmarii smiled softly. "It sounds like you are close to her."

"She is kind." Kayko nodded, his expression warmed, and he switched into mental conversation. *Lanikai has been secretly training me since I was able to walk. We used to sneak off and train. I thought I would want to be her Yutki partner, but now...* He hesitated, his eyes intentionally raised to meet Kilmarii's. *Now I think I would rather it be you.*

Kilmarii blinked, her heart lifted at his words. *Me?*

The two started the journey to the upper deck.

Yes, Kayko added a flash memory of Kilmarii

looking over at him as she unlatched the whale harness. *We worked so well together yesterday when we released the whale, and with Ouray. You are almost as strong and smart as me.* He paused, searching for the right words, and added, *We are family.*

A genuine smile spread across Kilmarii's face. *I would like that too, Kayko. I trust you.*

Kayko's grin grew brighter, his excitement nearly spilling over. *Then it is settled. We are partners.*

Their moment was interrupted as Tesi approached, carrying her bowls, her steps quick and filled with energy. "Good morning!" she greeted in Esor, her face lighting up. "May I join you?"

"Of course," Kayko said, as he slid over to make space.

Tesi placed her bowls down and beamed as she spoke, "I have been chosen as a Yutki! Maleia chose me last night." Her voice carried both nervousness and excitement. "I have been dreaming of this forever."

"We will all do great," Kilmarii assured her in Esor, her voice calm and encouraging. "Everyone feels nervous on their first day."

"Well, I am glad I am not alone," Tesi said with a laugh, "but you two already seem accepted as Yutkis already. People are talking about you, you know."

Kayko raised an eyebrow. "Oh? What are they saying?"

Tesi smirked as she replied, "They are saying that you are impressive, releasing Kaiyah from her harness, yesterday. I should stick close to you if I want to keep up."

Kayko chuckled, puffing his chest out playfully. "Well, they are not wrong. We are a fantastic team."

"You could join us," Kilmarii offered warmly. "We can help you learn the Yutki language too."

Tesi's eyes widened. "Really? That would be amazing. I only know a few words."

Their camaraderie grew, and they exchanged laughter as the ship creaked and swayed beneath them.

The three sat at the table, their bowls nearly emptied, laughter still passing between them. As Tesi leaned back, her smile changed into something more reflective.

"Do you remember, Kayko," Tessi began, her voice quiet and warm, "when we were little? We'd climb all over Jek?"

Kayko's grin slowly expanded at the memory; his voice carried a mix of amusement and nostalgia. He sent memories over to Kilmarii, as he responded directly to Tessi, "Of course I do. He would let us ride him."

Tesi laughed, her eyes sparkling. "I'll never forget the time he decided he was tired of carrying us and just lay down in the middle of the garden."

Kayko chuckled, shaking his head. "And Tozi had to come out and bribe him with handfuls of worms to get him to move."

Kilmarii The Wayfinder

"She was so mad at us for stomping through her plants!" Tesi added, giggling. "But she still let us help her afterward. Do you remember?"

Kayko nodded, his expression softened. "Yeah, we made a mess of things, but she just smiled and fixed it after we left."

"I was so sad when you stopped coming home, though," Tesi said, her tone shifted, her voice quieter. "After… after your mother died."

Kayko's smile faltered for the briefest moment, and his hand gripped around the edge of his bowl. The sound of Tesi's words seemed to echo in his mind, pulling him backward into memories he'd tried to bury.

Kilmarii let out a gasp as she received unintentional memories from Kayko - *The screams. The blood in the water. His mother's desperate cry as the shark tore her away.*

The image burned bright and raw, and Kayko felt his throat tighten. He forced a swallow, his face composed, but his eyes glazed over slightly as the memories gripped him.

Kilmarii's dark eyes filled with tears as she once again received the storm of emotion flashing through Kayko's mind. The weight of his pain, sharp and unfiltered, pressed into her chest like a stone. Without realizing it, a tear slipped down her cheek.

Tesi noticed the sudden change in the atmosphere; her face clouded with concern. She looked from Kilmarii to Kayko, her voice soft. "I'm sorry," she said, her words thick with guilt. "I didn't mean to bring up anything painful."

Kayko blinked, snapping back to the present. He shook his head quickly, his grin returned, though it didn't quite reach his eyes. "It's nothing," he said, his tone light and dismissive. "Really, it's fine. That was a long time ago."

Kilmarii wiped her tears away silently, watching him closely. He was pretending, she concluded, the raw ache still lingered at the edges of his thoughts.

Tesi leaned forward, her hand touched his. "Are you sure? I didn't mean to—"

"Tesi," Kayko interrupted, his grin widening, "you are very kind." He picked up the shell he'd been playing with earlier, flipping it deftly between his fingers, "I...we have Yutki training to focus on."

She said softly, offering him a small smile, "But if you ever want to talk with someone who remembers her well…"

"I appreciate it," Kayko said quickly, his voice warm but firm, redirecting the conversation. He turned to Kilmarii, his expression brightening. "Speaking of exciting, did I mention we might get to swim with the whales today?"

Kilmarii smiled faintly, her eyes still searching his, but she nodded. "That's something to look forward to," she said, her voice steady, choosing not to press him.

"Exactly!" Kayko exclaimed, his enthusiasm rising again as he clapped his hands together. "And

Kilmarii The Wayfinder

Tesi, you are going to love it. Swimming, fishing, working with whales."

The shift in tone pulled Tesi back into the present as well, her smile growing genuine again. "I can't wait," she said, her excitement bubbling up once more. "I had thought my place was going to be farming in the highlands. I always wanted to be out there with the whales, guiding the fish, hunting in the water like you."

Kayko leaned back, tossing the shell lightly into the air and catching it. "Then let's make this day unforgettable," he declared, his grin finally reaching his eyes again.

Kilmarii watched him closely, her own heart aching at the weight he carried. She resolved silently to be the partner he needed, someone who would share in his joy but help shoulder his pain.

Kayko, Kilmarii, and Tesi finished the last bites of their meal. The warm camaraderie between them lingered, their laughter tapering into quiet smiles.

A commanding voice sliced through the murmured conversations. "Yutki' trainees, attention!" Malka's tone was crisp and no-nonsense, immediately silencing the chatter in the dining area. All eyes turned toward her as she stood tall, her dark hair pulled back into a neat braid, her posture exuding authority.

Kayko's grin vanished in an instant, replaced by eager determination. He nudged Kilmarii with his elbow and stood. "That's our call," he said, his voice low and buzzing with anticipation.

Kilmarii nodded, rising smoothly to her feet. Tesi, still clutching her bowl, hesitated for a moment before quickly following their lead. The three moved toward Malka, joining the other Yutki trainees already gathering near her. There were seven in total: Kayko, Kilmarii, Tesi, and four other boys. They formed a loose semicircle around Malka, their body language revealing their nervous excitement.

Malka's sharp eyes swept over the group, lingering briefly on each trainee. "Now it's time to begin. Your journey as Yutki starts today, and with it comes responsibility and dedication to your clan, to the whales, to the ocean, and to each other."

Kayko straightened, his chest puffing slightly with pride. Kilmarii stood a little closer to him, her hands fidgeting with the edge of her tunic, though her eyes shone with eagerness.

Lanikai and Kayloni stepped forward to join Malka, their presence adding a sense of gravity to the moment. Lanikai offered the group a reassuring smile, her calm energy grounding the trainees. Kayloni, her expression focused, carried a small bundle of leather straps.

"We'll start with an introduction to the basics," Malka continued, her tone leaving no room for distraction. "How to guide fish into nets, how to care for the whales, and how to communicate with the ocean itself. These are skills brought to us by Maleia, Leader of the Yutki."

The trainees exchanged glances, a ripple of

excitement passed through them. Kayko glanced at Kilmarii, his eyes sparkling. "Ready?" he whispered, his voice barely audible.

Kilmarii nodded, a small smile tugging at her lips. "Always," she murmured back. Behind her mind shield, she was reviewing all the things her father had taught her.

Malka clapped her hands sharply, pulling their attention back to her. "Follow us," she commanded, her voice carrying an edge of expectation. "Your first lesson begins now."

The salty breeze carried a sense of adventure as the group watched as Malka stepped to the edge of the ship. She glanced back at the trainees, her commanding presence quieting any lingering chatter. Without a word, she dove gracefully into the ocean, her form cutting through the waves with practiced ease. Lanikai and Kayloni followed next. Kayko was the first trainee to follow them, his excitement infectious.

The water around them was alive with motion. Schools of fish darted past, their scales shimmering like liquid silver. Kilmarii's entire body came back to life, as she marveled at the energy permeating the waters of these islands. The kelp beds' synchronized movements and hearing the faint whispers of the others' thoughts as they wove around her was mesmerizing. A flash of green and brown caught her eye. It was a sea turtle nibbling at the translucent body of a jellyfish. She sensed its satisfaction, a contentment that echoed her own connection to the ocean.

Kayko swam ahead, his strokes powerful and even, keeping pace with the instructors. He flashed a grin over his shoulder at Kilmarii, who was easily keeping pace.

Kilmarii smirked and pushed harder, her muscles burning pleasantly with the effort. But as she glanced back, she noticed Tesi lagging behind. Her strokes were uneven, her face pinched with concentration. Kilmarii slowed and swam closer, trying to help her pace her strokes.

Ahead, Kayko swam alongside Malka, his movements mirroring hers with surprising precision. Malka glanced at him, her expression approving. Lanikai and Kayloni moved with the same admirable strength, a testament to years of training.

Kilmarii felt a subtle shift in the water, a ripple that brushed against her mind more than her body. Her senses stretched, touching the larger presences below. Whales, their immense forms moving slowly in the depths, their thoughts a distant, melodic hum. She felt their awareness, their curiosity, and their calm acceptance of the humans above.

She searched the minds of the others to find that Kayloni was also aware of the whales. But beneath the soothing melody of the whales, there was a sharper, more primal presence. A predator's mind brushed hers, its focus intense and singular. *Boaric.* Her heart quickened, though she forced herself to remain composed. She did not dare project her awareness too openly, wary of alerting Ouray who was always in range to monitor her thoughts. She sent a silent inquiry, and the shark's response was immediate; a flash of acknowledgment, raw and visceral. Boaric was watching, following, his presence unnerving as she recognized he was hunting.

The island rose ahead, a cluster of large rocks smoothed by the relentless tides and the force of countless storms. They gleamed in the sunlight, the surfaces polished to a soft shine by the ceaseless motion of the ocean. The trainees swam through the warm, crystal-clear water, their strokes smooth and rhythmic. Beneath them, the ocean was alive with vibrant coral, swaying seaweed, and darting schools of fish. Small rays glided lazily along the sandy bottom, while clusters of shellfish anchored themselves to the larger stones. The clarity of the water revealed a bustling underwater world teeming with abundant life in these sacred waters, known as the nursery.

Kilmarii reflected on the words her father shared when they fled to this bay to hide from her fate. He had shared that the ocean nursery was teaming with birth and flourishing with life, but it also attracted the great hunters, and therefore, it was also fraught with danger.

Kilmarii pulled her emotional thoughts back into check. She swam with purpose, her eyes taking in the underwater spectacle. She noticed Kayko up ahead, swimming effortlessly alongside Malka,

Lanikai, and Kayloni, his movements steadfast and strong. Tesi, once again, lagged slightly behind. Kilmarii slowed her pace, falling back to swim beside Tesi, offering silent encouragement with her steady presence.

The exhausted group reached the shore and pulled themselves onto the warm, sunlit rocks. The stones were solid underfoot, their smooth surfaces warmed from the sun. Between the larger formations, tidal pools glimmered in the sunlight, their clear water offering glimpses of trapped tiny fish, crabs, and sea urchins.

Kayloni gestured to one of the pools, her voice steady and instructive, "This is where we begin," she said, pointing to the darting shapes of small fish. "To control fish, you must learn to connect with them. Without the use of your hands to guide their movements, gently but firmly, direct their energy so that they move together in a circle, without causing harm."

The trainees gathered around the tidal pool and kneeled on the smooth stones to watch Kayloni demonstrate. Kilmarii sat beside Kayko, her fingers skimming the surface of the water as she watched the fish below. Kayloni crouched next to the pool, but not in the water, demonstrating the technique. Her hands moved fluidly, forming the shape of a circle just above the surface of the water. The movements seemed to coax the fish into the synchronized pattern.

"Like this," Kayloni said, her tone encouraging.

Kilmarii The Wayfinder

"Feel their energy, their movements. It is important to develop the ability to guide them to make the movement of their own free will, and not force them."

As Kayloni spoke, Kayko translated into Esor for Tesi. It was a gesture of kindness that Kilmarii noticed.

"Let's go around in a circle as well." She gestured for one of the boys to begin.

One by one, the trainees took turns, their hands hovering above the water with varying levels of confidence. Kayko's movements earned a quick response from the fish, the tiny creatures darting into a loose spiral before settling again. Tesi, her brows knit in concentration, mimicked Kayloni's gestures, her success met with an encouraging nod from the instructor.

Kilmarii waited for her turn, observing each movement closely. When her hands hovered above the water, she felt a subtle connection, a quiet awareness of the fish as they gathered under her hand. She focused, her movements deliberate and measured. Slowly, the fish began to circle, their tiny bodies aligning to form a visible current in the pool. Then Kilmarii lowered her cupped hands into the water, and the school of tiny fish crowded onto her palms.

"Excellent," Kayloni said, her voice warm with approval, "you have a natural enchantment, Kilmarii."

The lesson continued until the sun was at its

highest point overhead, and the shadows disappeared from the rocks. The trainees, now more confident, worked in small groups, practicing their skills together under the watchful eyes of Malka, Lanikai, and Kayloni. The tidal pool glimmered with activity as the trainees refined their techniques, their laughter and determination filling the air.

That evening at the knower meeting, as in every knower meeting held thereafter on that journey, Kayko relayed the lessons of the day to the rest of the members. Maleia led most meetings, and Kilmarii listened in through the open channel of mind stream that Ouray offered her. To disguise what she was up to, Kilmarii would often pretend to be asleep, resting between Yutki training and the nightly clan meeting.

Chapter Fourteen

Mind Shielding

The night sky was still painted with stars when Kayko stirred from his sleep. The moon hung low on the horizon, its soft glow filtered through the wooden slats of the ship deck above.

A firm mental nudge from Jyukan reached him, followed by Tozi's calm voice in his mind telling him to come to her.

Wake up, children. Come quietly to my room. Be sure not to alert humans or animals.

Kayko sat up, rubbing his eyes, and glanced at Kilmarii, who was already stirring, sensing the same mental call. Both children moved silently, careful not to disturb the others sleeping in the common room. The soft creak of the ship's boards under their feet was the only sound as they made

Lisa Newton

their way toward Tozi's quarters.

When they entered, Tozi and Jyukan were already seated in a circle, their faces serious. Tozi gestured for them to sit.

Tonight is important, Jyukan began.

We will teach you the skill of mind shielding that has not been necessary in our family for generations, but is now vital.

Kayko's brows furrowed, his heart began to race, as he sat cross-legged on the floor. *Mind shielding? I thought our open minds made us stronger as a family.*

Tozi nodded, her expression warm but firm. *In our small family, yes. We have always worked as one. But there are threats now that require you to protect your thoughts and emotions, not only from other knowers but also from animals and fish.*

Why now? Kayko asked, his face showing a hint of unease.

Jyukan leaned forward slightly to be sure they understood. *Because your talents are growing. And because others may not always have your best interests at heart.*

Tozi's gaze shifted to Kilmarii. *Ouray has shared with us that you already possess advanced skills in shielding your mind, and perhaps even more advanced than any of us here.*

Kayko's eyes widened as he looked at his adopted sister, then he asked, *More advanced than Ouray?*

Tozi and I believe it is possible, Jyukan

Kilmarii The Wayfinder

confirmed, *However, Kilmarii still has much to learn, particularly about reading memories. That skill is rare. Only Mato and Ouray mastered it fully. Tozi and I can manage it with animals and fish, but are limited when it comes to human minds; as are you, Kayko.*

Comprehending Kayko's conflicted emotions, Tozi's voice softened, "This is not to diminish your gifts, Kayko. You, too, have great potential. Your connection to the animals, especially the whales, is unique and powerful."

Kayko nodded slowly, digesting the information. *How do we start?*

Close your eyes, Tozi instructed and lowered herself, so she sat directly behind Kayko. She placed her hands just beside each of his ears. *Picture your face. This is your first shield. It will protect your thoughts and emotions.*

Jyukan sat behind Kilmarii and extended his hands beside her ears as well. The children obeyed, their faces reflected their intense concentration as they tried to follow the guidance. Jyukan and Tozi demonstrated their mental walls becoming visible to the children as faint, shimmering barriers that could only be observed in the shared mind stream.

You must also learn to extend this shield outward, Jyukan continued, *so that animals and fish cannot sense your presence. This is especially important when you are near predators.*

Kilmarii nodded, her face thoughtful. *I have done this with humans before. It helps when I need to move among them without causing alarm.*

Tozi's eyes flickered with curiosity. *Tell us more.*

Tozi moved so she could face Kilmarii and took her hands in hers.

Kilmarii hesitated but then began to provide details.

When I was a child, my father taught me to survive in the ocean. My people did not train me because I was not going to be selected. They had always planned to remove me.

Her voice wavered slightly but steadied as she continued.

My father showed great affection for me and wanted me to live. He was the one who taught me to shield myself, to care for the creatures of the sea. My father trained me to hunt, to listen, to survive.

Her words came with images, and the flashes of her past were shared through the connections of the mind stream. A memory of her father guiding her small hands as she wove a net. Another of her swimming alongside a young shark, its movements playful and curious.

Kayko flinched as an image came through clearly: Kilmarii and Boaric, her shark companion, were hunting together. His expression hardened, and he pulled back from the shared stream.

You... You are not a shark fighter, Kayko managed to choke out his response, his face showing disbelief. *You are a caretaker of sharks?*

Kilmarii admitted, her tone unapologetic, *I care*

Kilmarii The Wayfinder

for them. *I understand them just as you do the other animals of the ocean. That is why I can do what I do. I have been taught, just as you have, our place in this world.*

Jyukan interjected, *This is her gift, Kayko. Do not resent it. Kilmarii's skills make her unique amongst our clan, just as your connection to the whales makes you Kayloni's equal.*

Kayko's blood boiled, and his jaw tightened, but he nodded reluctantly.

Tozi reached out physically, offering reassurance to both children.

This is a time for understanding and growth. Do not let fear or doubt cloud your bond.

Kilmarii smiled shyly at Tozi and Jyukan, her eyes filled with tears.

I will share more when you ask. I promise. But I have much to learn, and I need a family. More tears flowed steadily down her cheeks.

Jyukan placed a hand on her shoulder, his touch reassuring.

We are here to guide you, both of you. Together, we will ensure you are prepared for whatever lies ahead.

The lesson continued, the children practicing their shields under the careful watch of their elders. By the end of the session, the tension from Kayko towards Kilmarii remained behind his mind shield.

As they left Tozi's room, the ocean's gentle rhythm filled the silence between them. Kayko walked a few paces ahead, his thoughts swirling with resentment.

Kilmarii followed quietly, her mind focused on the newfound clarity of sharing her truths with her adopted family.

For Kayko, the sunrise felt heavy for the first time.

Chapter Fifteen

Sharks of All Forms

Malka was the first to reach the shore, pulling herself up onto the rocks with practiced ease. She turned to observe the trainees as they arrived, her sharp eyes noting every movement.

Kayko climbed onto the rocks next, his grin wide and triumphant. He shook water from his hair, glancing back to watch Kilmarii and Tesi approach. Kilmarii reached out to steady Tesi as they clambered onto the stones together. Tesi's hands trembled slightly, but she gave Kilmarii a grateful smile.

"You did it," Kilmarii said softly, her tone warm with encouragement.

Tesi nodded, still catching her breath. "Thanks to you."

"Everyday you improve."

Malka's voice cut through the sound of the waves.

"It is time."

Her glare swept over them, lingering briefly on each face. Her sisters nodded in approval.

"Today, we begin with a lesson in communication," she announced with authority. "The ocean teems with life, and as Yutkis, it is your responsibility to understand it. To guide it. To protect it. And yes, to hunt it."

Malka watched them closely, her expression unreadable. "Good. Our lesson today will focus on how to protect from sharks," her face now revealed the seriousness she felt.

The ocean felt alive around them, a vibrant tapestry of sound, movement, and thought. As the trainees worked, a sense of unity began to form—a bond not just between them, but with the world they were learning to command.

The sun climbed higher in the sky, its warmth mingling with the salty tang of the air. Kilmarii looked out at the ocean, her awareness brushing briefly against Boaric's presence. He lingered on the edge of her senses, a silent observer.

The trainees gathered on the sun-warmed rocks. Fresh water had been left for them along with some fruit. Kayloni stepped forward to begin the next lesson. The ocean breeze ruffled her dark hair, and

Kilmarii The Wayfinder

the sunlight glinted off the small bundle she carried of shark egg cases. Her expression was serious as she gestured for everyone to sit.

The group settled on the stones, forming a half-circle around her. Kayko leaned forward, his elbows on his knees, his eagerness apparent. Kilmarii sat cross-legged, reading the apprehension in the fidgeting Tesi. She focused unsuccessfully to read Kayko but was met with his shield.

Kayloni lifted one of the eggs, holding it up for the group to see. "Today," she began, "we are learning about sharks. These predators are not only dangerous but also incredibly unpredictable. We must be vigilant at all times, and as Yutkis, we must also know how to protect ourselves and the whales."

She paused, letting her words sink in. "Sharks have different ways of having babies. Some give birth to live young. Others lay eggs that look like this." She shook the egg, and the trainees leaned closer to inspect it. "These are thick skins that hold shark eggs until the babies hatch."

Kilmarii tilted her head, the presence of Boaric drew her attention. Her connection to him felt suddenly complicated, and she pushed the feeling aside, focusing only on Kayloni's words.

"Some sharks give birth to live babies. It is these types of sharks that some of us have the ability to sense."

Kayloni continued, holding up a dead baby shark for the trainees to observe.

Tesi interrupted. "Why does it matter how

sharks have babies?"

Kayloni's expression hardened as she addressed the question. "It matters because we are unable to sense this kind of shark." Once again, she was holding the dead baby shark up above her head. "Knowing which kind of shark helps us understand how to protect ourselves and the whales."

"Sharks that lay eggs hide them on the seabed, like these." She gestured to the shark egg in her hand. "If we find and destroy the eggs, it can stop more sharks from being born. Sharks that give birth live are harder to stop, but knowing the difference helps us plan."

Kilmarii listened closely, she was glad that Kayko was shielded and wouldn't know that she was warning Boaric. She knew she would have to hide her connection to him from Kayko and the others.

Kayloni rose, brushing sand from her hands. "Now we are going to look for shark eggs. If you find an egg, stab all the way through it with your spear, then bring it to me. If you see a baby shark, call for help. Do not approach it alone." Her tone grew firmer with each word. "This is serious work. Be cautious and alert."

The trainees nodded and grabbed a spear from the pile, the weight of the task settling over them. Kayloni led the group toward the shallow tide pools that dotted the shoreline. The sun glimmered on the water's surface, and tiny fish scattered as they approached. Kayko took the lead, his sharp eyes scanning under the surface for baby sharks, while Kilmarii and Tesi followed close behind.

Tesi crouched beside Kilmarii, her brow furrowed with concentration. "Do you think we will find anything?" she whispered.

"Maybe," Kilmarii replied quietly. Her eyes flicked to a cluster of rocks where a dark shape caught her attention.

Tesi reached out carefully, her fingers closing around a small, leathery case tangled in seaweed.

"I found one!" Tesi yelled as she held the egg case up. The texture was smooth against her skin. The others gathered around, their curiosity palpable.

Kayloni approached, her expression approving. "Good work, Tesi. That is one." She took it from Tesi's hand, tossed it to the sand, and impaled it with her spear. "This one would have hatched soon. You did well to find it."

Kayloni and Lanikai leaned against the same rock, the gentle warmth of the stone radiating through their tired backs. Kayloni squatted down, her eyes scanning where the waves lapped against the shore. Deep in discussion, they shared observations from the recent Yutki training.

"Kayko and Tesi are excelling," Lanikai offered. "Their partnership is seamless. Kayko's strength and leadership complement Tesi's focus and precision. They meet every task we set for them."

Kayloni nodded thoughtfully. "Agreed. But the same cannot be said for Ren and Tarkan. They are stumbling, unable to balance. Their strengths are not aligned."

Lanikai tilted her head, her expression thoughtful. "What if we replaced one of them? Kilmarii has shown remarkable skills. She has strong communication skills with all ocean animals, she is adept at diving, and fearless."

Without hesitation, Kayloni agreed, "I too think she has great skills, but you know that is impossible. Mother has decided Kilmarii must work alone."

"What our mother said is what will be, but it is not our choice," Lanikai protested, her voice rising slightly in frustration. "We are the instructors. We should be able to decide what is best for the trainees."

Kayloni sighed, with a cheeky smirk, looked up at her sister, "It is not a fight worth having. Mother's will is final, and you know it."

Nearby, Kayko and Kilmarii crouched over a tidal pool, playing a battle between Kayko's fish and Kimarii's. Both overheard the conversation; the words sat heavily on Kilmarii.

"Looks like you really are meant to be alone," he teased aloud, his tone sharp enough to sting.

Kilmarii's eyes stalled for a moment, her face frozen in time, and a panic started to rise within her. She said nothing, focusing instead on her task, but Kayko felt the weight of her hurt pressing against his mind. He frowned, regret washing over him.

"I am sorry," he said quickly, his voice softening. "I did not mean it."

Kilmarii The Wayfinder

Kayko hesitated before adding, *You are better than me, you know. I mean it. Everyone sees it, even if they do not say it.*

Kilmarii did not respond; instead, she withdrew behind an emotional shield by keeping her focus on the pool. Kayko sighed, his shoulders slumped slightly.

Kayloni gathered the trainees back to the rocks after their search through the tide pools. The sun was higher now, and the sea breeze carried the salty tang of the ocean. She waited until everyone was seated again, their earlier energy now tempered. Kayko sat cross-legged at the front, his eyes fixed on Kayloni with quiet intensity.

"Before we continue our hunt," Kayloni began, holding up the small shark egg Kilmarii found earlier, "I need you to understand why sharks are so drawn to us, to our ships, to our fish nets, and now here in the whale nursery."

She paused, letting the sound of waves fill the silence for a moment. "Sharks are hunters, but they are also survivors. Their habitat preferences and behavior are tied to their survival needs. Some sharks prefer the shallow, coastal areas, like this one." She gestured to the tidepools and rocky shoreline around them. "These places are full of prey and serve as nurseries for their young. Baby sharks are safer here than out in the open ocean."

Tesi raised her voice, "Does that mean there are always sharks nearby in this bay?"

Kayloni nodded affirmatively, "Often, yes.

Coastal areas provide food and protection, making them ideal for certain species. That is why we find eggs and baby sharks."

She stood and pointed to the horizon, where the vast blue stretched endlessly. "Some sharks live in the open ocean, far from land. These sharks travel great distances, following migratory routes and ocean currents. They hunt where the food is, and they are drawn to anything that might lead them to prey."

Kayko tilted his head, his curiosity evident. "Is that why they follow our ships? Because of the fish we catch?"

"Exactly," Kayloni affirmed. "When we fish with nets, we leave injured fish, causing the smell of blood in the water. That is why we process our fish on land. Sharks are incredibly sensitive to the smell of blood. They sense them from afar and follow, hoping for an easy meal. That is why we see so many when we hunt."

Kayloni's tone became more serious as she continued. "Currently, in this bay, it is even more dangerous. This place is a nursery for not just whales; it is the warm waters for many fish to birth and raise their young. But to sharks, it is an opportunity. Weak or newborn whales are easy targets, and the scent of birth carries in the water. That is why the big sharks are here."

Tesi's eyes narrowed, her voice lowered. "So, we are protecting the whales from the sharks?"

"Yes," Kayloni said firmly. "Our role as Yutkis

Kilmarii The Wayfinder

is to protect the whales, and hunt for fish and seals. We cannot let them harm the whales or disrupt them. Our whales expect us to care for them, as they care for us."

Kayko frowned slightly, his hands resting on his knees. "The sharks' presence threatens our clan; we must act."

Kilmarii turned away from Kayko, she was able to discern that the rest of the Yutkis admired his sentiments. She felt the emotions welling up in Kayloni, Malka, and Lanikai, as his mother had been one of their Yutki hunting instructors.

Kayloni straightened, her mind shifting to one of purpose. "Now, we are going to put this knowledge into action. I want you to think about the movements of the fish you guided earlier. Imagine how you might use those same techniques to avoid sharks. How would one drive them away or disrupt their hunting patterns?"

She picked up a small stick and drew a simple diagram in the sand. "This is how sharks move when they hunt. They circle their prey, testing for weakness. If you see this behavior, you must work together to protect the whales or drive the sharks away. Use your minds to create confusion with fish, to disrupt their focus."

Kayko leaned forward, his mind brightened by determination, "Can we try it now?"

Kayloni's smile faded, "Not in open water, yet. First, we will practice many more days within the tide pools. Then, when all are ready, we will partner you with experienced Yutkis to hunt in the open ocean. We must protect you all as you learn under close supervision. After all, we do wish to add you all to our Yutki ranks."

Tesi leaned into Kilmarii, her signal to get a discreet translation into Esor.

The trainees exchanged acknowledgment, a mix of excitement and dread rippled through the group. Tesi raised her spear above her head. "Let's go!"

"Spear the eggs," Kayloni instructed, "and if you see a live baby, make sure the mother shark is not around, then kill it. I will be close by if you want to call for help. If you are not ready, do not try to handle it alone."

The group nodded, their focus sharpening as they rose to their feet.

They worked together to reduce the shark population until the sun was low in the sky. As the day came to a close, Malka stepped onto the largest rock; her commanding presence drew the group's attention. The trainees gathered below her, their faces flushed with the day's effort, and glowing with pride.

"You have all done well today," Malka announced, her voice carrying over the gentle sound of the waves. "Tomorrow, we will continue to build on what you have learned. Kilmarii, we noticed you did not kill today. Perhaps your reputation as a shark hunter has been exaggerated?"

Not one to stand down from an insult, Kilmarii dared to speak out, "I don't see a purpose in killing something so young if it is not eaten."

In a tone that matched the disgust on his face, Kayko retorted, "We don't eat shark. The flesh is sour." If eyes could wound, his would have speared Kilmarii.

Malka continued, "For now, we will assign your partners. This will be the person you will train with, learn with, and work alongside as you grow into your roles as Yutkis." She began calling out names, pairing each trainee. When she reached Kayko's name, she paused, her eyes landing on Kilmarii before she continued, "Kayko, your partner will be Tesi."

Kayko was surprised but quickly nodded, offering Tesi an encouraging smile.

Tesi, clearly pleased, cast a fleeting glance at Kilmarii, her excitement untempered by her unexpected partnership.

Malka's voice took on a more solemn tone as she concluded, "Kilmarii, you will not have a partner at this time. Your training will be handled separately."

A loud murmur of surprise passed through the group. Kayko's eyes widened, and he opened his mouth as if to speak, but a poke in the back from Kayloni silenced him, as he read her thoughts to learn Malka and Maleia were going to break Kilmarii's spirit. He turned to evaluate how Kilmarii was reacting to the news, if she too had also entered their minds and read their intentions.

He let down his shield to connect with Kilmarii.

Kilmarii's face remained composed, though a flicker of emotion passed through her eyes. She nodded, her chin lifting slightly in quiet acceptance. Her shield was up, and she did not answer his mental call.

"That is all for today," Malka finished, stepping down from her perch. "Rest well. Tomorrow will be another demanding day."

The trainees dispersed slowly, their earlier camaraderie tinged with a mix of curiosity and unease. Kayko lingered near Kilmarii as they made their way back to the water. He was determined to have her learn his opinion, if not by sharing minds then by using his voice.

"I do not understand why you are being separated," he said, his brows furrowed. "You did better than all of us."

Kilmarii was furious inside, but she would never allow Kayko the pleasure of knowing it. She offered a small smile and used her voice, "Perhaps there is something else I need to learn."

As they slipped back into the warm, clear water, the group swam back to the ships for the night. The ocean embraced them, its life-filled depths a reminder of the challenges and wonders that lay ahead.

Kilmarii swam with purpose, her mind reliving the moment, briefly feeling unsteady and insecure. She punished her emotions with a hard swim, and by the time she reached the ladder, she was determined to meet whatever came next with strength and grace.

With Kilmarii listening intently from her bed, the knowers' meeting had begun, and through the mind stream she knew Maleia sat at the center.

"This evening," Maleia announced, her tone measured and deliberate, "we solidify the partnerships of our Yutki trainees. These bonds will guide their training and future contributions to the clan."

She turned to Jyukan, her Yutki partner, offering him a rare, pleasant smile. Her attention shifted to Kayko. "Kayko, I trust you are pleased to be partnered with your childhood friend Tesi?"

Kayko hesitated only the briefest of moments, the weight of his unspoken disappointment pressing down on him. He forced a small smile, but before he could respond, his father Jyukan's mental voice reached him.

Keep your thoughts to yourself, son. The clan must see unity, not discord.

Tozi's mental voice followed, calm and reassuring. *It is important to protect Kilmarii's role. Let Maleia believe this arrangement serves her interests.*

Kayko couldn't shake the dismay he felt deep inside. Maleia studied his face, her keen eyes narrowing. "You do not seem as happy as I would have expected," she said, her tone curious and bitterly sharp. "Why is that, Kayko?"

Kayko drew a deep breath.

"I am grateful to have Tesi as my partner," he

said. "She is my friend, and we have shared many good memories. But…" his gaze flickered toward his father. "I had expected to be paired with my new sister. We work well together."

Maleia's lips pressed into a thin line as she pretended to comfort him, her tone softened insincerely.

"It is natural to wish for what is familiar, Kayko," she said. "But Kilmarii's role is too unique for her to be an ordinary Yutki. She will hold the new position of shark defender, created specifically for her talents."

The room fell into a heavy silence, though the mental conversation between the knowers carried on, weaving beneath the surface of Maleia's spoken words. Maleia, oblivious to the silent exchange, continued, her voice laced with a satisfaction that bordered on condescension.

This position will keep her hidden, Tozi projected calmly. *It allows her to train away from scrutiny.*

And it assures she spends more time with you and Ouray, Jyukan added.

"Kilmarii's ability to command sharks is rare and invaluable. She will serve the clan in ways no other can. And, of course," Maleia added with a faint smirk, "it is a dangerous role. Only the strongest can manage it."

Jyukan rose to his feet, his expression composed as he addressed both Maleia and the silent knowers.

"I am pleased that Kilmarii has found her place

within the clan," he said firmly, his tone carried layers of meaning.

Maleia nodded, satisfied with his response. She scanned the faces in the room, her posture easing. Beneath her calm exterior, Maleia felt a swell of unease rise from her decision. Kilmarii, she believed, would either prove her worth or fall victim to the dangers of her role. Either way may be a victory for the Yutki clan.

Kilmarii continued pretending to rest on her bedroll and remained silent as she listened to the currents of mental conversation on the other side of the wall. She knew of the support of Jyukan and Tozi, their steady belief in her abilities bolstering her resolve not to fall victim to melancholy.

"Ouray has decided to remain at the shore camp," Maleia announced next, her voice steady and deliberate. "He will not rejoin us at these meetings until it is time to begin the journey home."

The air grew immediately tense, and a rapid exchange of unspoken thoughts passed through the gathered knowers. Kayko stiffened slightly, his eyes flickering with questions he could never voice.

"This means," Maleia continued, her tone even and firm, "that the Nek training for Kayko and Kilmarii will no longer proceed as planned. Ouray has other priorities that demand his attention."

Tozi shifted uncomfortably, her hands curling into fists at her sides. "He did not share this with me!" she blurted, her tone tinged openly with frustration. "Ouray was teaching them important skills. Why would he stop now, and why would Jyukan and I not be told this by our brother directly?"

Maleia's sharp eyes settled on Tozi, and her expression remained calm, though there was a finality in her voice. "Ouray feels his time is better spent preparing to lead the trade exchange. The clan has other needs that take precedence over individual instruction."

Kayko pressed his lips together, glancing at his father, Jyukan, and his aunt Tozi for support. A silent conversation unfolded in the mental stream between them. Tozi's mind stirred with frustration, but Jyukan's calming influence kept her from speaking again. She nodded in apparent acceptance, though her disappointment was clearly known to the others, including Kilmarii.

"The focus now," Maleia continued, "must remain on ensuring the safety and success of our journey. Each of you has a role to play, and I expect nothing less than your full commitment."

Jyukan inclined his head in acknowledgment. "Of course. We are all dedicated to the success of the clan, as always."

Once more, Maleia's eyes scanned the group, her posture exuding authority, "Good. I trust each of you to fulfill your responsibilities."

As the meeting concluded, the knowers began to disperse. Tozi sent out a message to Ouray. *This does not feel right.*

There was no response from Ouray.

Kilmarii The Wayfinder

Tozi asked Jyukan, *Try to reach Ouray for confirmation of his plans.*

Jyukan tried and failed, *Ouray does not respond. I do not sense him. He must be out of our range.*

Why couldn't he just have his shield up? Inquired Kilmarii, who is now on the deck, looking from the rail of the ship towards the shore camp.

Jyukan answered her, *He has never done so in the past. He doesn't feel it necessary to keep anything from us.*

Kilmarii sent out her own call to Ouray. Nothing returned.

Jyukan placed a reassuring hand on Kayko's shoulder, *We all adapt, Kayko. The clan's needs come first. Trust that what you have learned so far will serve you well.*

Tozi stepped closer, her voice calm and encouraging, *You have grown much already, Kayko. There will always be more to learn, even when the path ahead seems unclear.* She added, *Perhaps it is time for you both to learn from me?*

Kayko nodded reluctantly, his young face a mix of determination and disappointment. As the group dissolved into the night, the ocean's steady rhythm filled the air, a reminder of the ever-changing tides and the challenges that lay ahead.

As the meeting concluded, Maleia's contentment radiated outward. She gloated as she watched the gathered knowers silently walk up the ladder to the main deck.

At the clan meeting, Maleia announced that the trade journey had begun, and Ouray and Pare had already begun the trading negotiations with other water traveling clans at the southern shore of the bay. The clan members started to murmur and all eyes stole glances at Jyukan, who was the leader of the previous trade journeys. She then ordered the rest of the trading supplies to be placed into Ouray's ship vessels and rowed over to him at camp. When asked about animals to transport the supplies over land, Maleia explained they would need to use their skills as animal knowers and call horses or similar large animals. This would have seemed an impossible task, if Ouray's power to control animals was not known to the clan, but as it was known, the announcement made sense.

Then Maleia laughed loudly, "Or perhaps they may all find armadillos of their own to ride."

Kilmarii and Kayko nearly broke out into laughter, absorbing images projected of clan members riding armadillos that flowed freely from the clan.

As the meeting progressed, Jyukan locked his eyes on Maleia and remained silent.

Chapter Sixteen

Tozi's Childhood

The rhythmic sound of the ocean filled the dark room, waves lapping against the ship's hull, their gentle cadence weaving through the stillness. Tozi sat cross-legged on the floor, her mental voice carried through the night like a soft tide, weaving a story that drifted into the minds of the two children lying nearby.

When I was young, she began, her voice carrying the weight of memory, *my mind was open to all things. I heard the thoughts of every man, woman, and child. The birds spoke to me of their skyward flights; the fish whispered of deep currents. Every living creature, from the smallest insect to the largest whale, shared their voices with me, unceasing and overwhelming.*

The children, resting deeply, stirred faintly as her words painted their images in their minds. Kayko's body enveloped Kilmarii protectively.

At first, I thought it a blessing, she continued, her tone soothing. *But as time passed, the constant flood of words weighed on me. I could not find my own thoughts in the endless noise. Their stories, fears, and dreams crowded my mind, and I became lost. The burden hurt me deeply, more than anyone could see. Each voice pulled at my heart, leaving no room for my own.*

Outside, the waves rose and fell, their soothing rhythm underscoring her words. *When I was a child, I sought refuge in the water. Beneath its surface, where the world's noise faded, the voices of fish and whales sang to me in harmony with nature. Their melodies were pure and soothing, unlike the harsh din of the world above. In the water, I found a quiet I longed for. But when I returned to my people, the voices would rise again, filling me with their truths and unspoken motives.*

Her voice now carried a note of sadness. *Knowing the hearts of others left me feeling alone. I could not find friends, for I always understood too much—every fear, every secret, every reason behind their actions. Even the future revealed itself to me through the echoes of the past. And so, I wandered, seeking silence, yearning for peace that eluded me.*

The children, though still, felt the story wrap

Kilmarii The Wayfinder

around them, drawing them deeper into her words.

One day, Tozi continued, her voice trembling slightly, *I could bear it no longer. I walked to the roaring river, where the waters rushed fiercely between the rocks, their currents unrelenting. I let myself fall into the torrent, my body carried toward the crushing embrace of the stones. I thought it would end there, that the river would take me, and with it, the unbearable noise.*

The room seemed to hold its breath. Tozi's voice weakened into a thread of a whisper, *But as I surrendered to the current, I felt myself lifted. Not by hands, not by a force I could see, but by something greater. The river released me, and I awoke in the medicine garden of my grandmother.*

She paused, *My grandmother, wise and kind, ran to me. She held her hands over my ears, and in that moment, she took away my ability to hear. It was the gift of silence. For the first time, my mind was my own. The voices faded, and I began to heal.*

Her words lingered in the air, heavy and profound, *Little by little, peace returned to me. With it came love and joy, filling the spaces once occupied by endless words. My heart became light again, and I found I could laugh and live fully. Eventually, I asked my grandmother to restore my knowing. I missed the sounds of the world of laughter, the songs, and most of all the communion of nature.*

She returned my hearing, but not as it had been before. She made it softer, less overwhelming, so I could hear when I wished and retreat into silence when I needed it. From that day, I learned to strengthen my mind shield, to find wisdom in listening and beauty in silence.

Her voice lingered in the air, light like a butterfly in flight. *And now I tell you this, my little ones: you hold the power to grow your silence, to protect your minds and open them only when it is right. Silence is not emptiness. It is a wellspring of peace, a space where your own thoughts can flourish. And when you choose to listen fully, you will find wisdom waiting for you.*

The waves outside seemed to swell gently, their sounds blending with the stillness of the night. The children's faces remained peaceful as her story settled into their dreams, like the gentle ebb and flow of the tide. She rose quietly, walking to join them in the next room. Tozi remained between the children and Jyukan. Her thoughts called out to Ouray, *Return to us.*

***

The days stretched long and lonely, oppressing the spirit of Kilmarii. Though her performance in training often surpassed that of the other trainees, the praise always seemed to fall on Kayko. Worse still, the group's dynamics had shifted against her. The trainees excluded her from conversations and whispered cruel remarks when they thought she could not hear. Her budding friendship with Tesi

Kilmarii The Wayfinder

died.

Even Kayko, bowing to peer pressure, joined in the teasing during the day. But at night, when the family gathered for their stories and lessons with Jyukan and Tozi, he returned to his old self, often offering apologies for his behavior.

One evening, as they sat under the glow of the moon, Kayko leaned in toward her and spoke. "I am sorry for today." He whispered these words for the third night in a row, "I did not mean it."

Kilmarii snapped, her voice as sharp as she intended, "Stop apologizing, Kayko. Make up your mind. Are you my brother or not?" Several clan members turned in their direction, taking notice of the unusual exchange.

Kayko blinked, stunned into silence. Her words hung heavy in the air, cutting through his excuses. He looked away, his mind churning with guilt.

Later that night, Jyukan pulled Kayko aside and asked him to walk the deck with him.

Do you know what happens to people who are disloyal, Kayko? Who are intentionally cruel to the weaker?

Kayko lowered his head. *No.*

They grow up to be lonely men, shunned by those they tried to impress. Strength comes from kindness, not cruelty. Tozi and I are not able to follow you the way we once did, but you can never be far away enough or use your shield well enough to hide from your father. Do not let others decide who you are.

Kayko nodded solemnly, the weight of his father's words sinking in.

Kilmarii The Wayfinder

Chapter Seventeen

Perseverance

As the trainees neared the end of their program, they were paired with experienced Yutkis to learn the art of net fishing in the open ocean. They were to join in the task vital for resupplying the ships in preparation for the journey home. The bay was alive with activity as the clan prepared, collecting fresh water and food stores, while Maleia warned of changing weather.

Kilmarii worked tirelessly; her solo assignment kept her beneath the fishing boats as a shark defender. The waters remained shark-free, and the other clan members heaped praise on her efforts, recognizing her role in ensuring their safety.

For the first time in weeks, Kilmarii felt a belonging as the clan's gratitude reached her.

Lisa Newton

Jyukan and Tozi watched from a distance, sharing a quiet mental exchange.

She has earned her place, Jyukan said, his pride clear in his thoughts.

Tozi nodded, *Despite everything, she has proven herself. The others feel it now for they see her as one of us.*

Even Maleia, watching Kilmarii from afar, sensed the shift in the clan's perception of her. Though her lips curled into a smile, her thoughts gave much credit to her daughters' training, and she remained guarded about fully accepting Kilmarii. *Let her have her moment,* Maleia thought silently, *the journey home will bring new challenges.*

Kilmarii The Wayfinder

Chapter Eighteen

Prelude

The moon hung low in the sky, casting a soft silver glow. The stars scattered like glittering jewels, over the mirrored surface of the ocean. From the deck, the brittle creak of wood and the occasional whisper of the breeze were the only sounds breaking the night's serenity.

Inside the clan common room, Jyukan and Tozi sat cross-legged on thick pelts, deep in discussion and counting the supply knots. It was Tozi who cataloged and maintained a count of the clan's supplies stored on each ship. It fell on Jyukan, Ouray, and Maleia to organize the people. In their bedrolls were Kayko and Kilmarii, tired from their day, and waiting for their parental night's lesson to begin floating into their brains.

With her dark eyes alight with a mixture of excitement and mischief, Kilmarii poked Kayko in the ribs.

I have an idea. Kilmarii paused, looking between Jyukan and Tozi, measuring their reaction, *let's have an adventure.*

Jyukan raised an eyebrow, intrigued, *What kind of adventure?*

Kilmarii closed her eyes briefly; she could hardly believe her luck, as it seemed they were going to entertain her idea. She flooded the minds of the knowers with the most vivid memory visions she had ever sent them.

The images that come to life were sharks motionless on the sandy bottom of a luminous underwater cave, their sleek forms motionless. Hot bubbles rose lazily from the sand, traveling upward toward the shimmering surface.

The cave's upper walls gleamed with dazzling quartz crystal structures in hues of purple, blue, and taupe, their sharp edges refracting the light like stars. Above it all, the cave's fissure opened to the heavens, the stars framed perfectly by the crystalline edges.

Kilmarii's memories carried them under the water, through a cave, and surfacing in a small tide pool. Over the entrance to the cave, a massive stone sat solemnly, its surface marked by three spirals of geometrically perfect circles radiating outward from a central point. From the memory emanated a sacred feeling, the cave's beauty mingled with the

Kilmarii The Wayfinder

primal danger of the sleeping sharks.

Tozi gasped, breaking the silence. She heard the certainty in Kilmarii's voice, but what gripped her the most were the images she shared: the sharks resting peacefully, the crystals refracting light into something almost divine, the bubbling sands. It was beautiful but dangerous, and she felt the weight of Kilmarii's request settle on her shoulders.

Tozi remembered when she was younger, bolder, and full of quests like this. Her spirit called her back for a moment, wanting to believe she could still venture into the unknown.

This… this is the sacred Temple of the Water, Kilmarii's mental voice tinged with awe and reverence. *It is real. I have been there. If we combine all our skills, we can slip away tonight without being detected by animals, fish, or humans to see it for ourselves. We must go before it is too late. When Ouray and the trading party return, the whales will be called, and the ships will leave the bay.*

The risk is great. To leave the clan so unguarded... But even as the thought formed in Jyukan's mind, the allure of the memory gripped him. The vivid beauty, the adventure, the chance to use their combined powers—it stirred something youthful and rebellious within him.

Tozi responded, her tone thoughtful, "But I am no longer young. The swim may be too much."

You taught me how to swim, Jyukan said, looking at Tozi. *You taught me everything I know.*

And now you say you are too old?

Jyukan smiled, a warmth spreading through his mental voice. *You are the strongest among us, Tozi. Your spirit is as youthful as ever. You only need to remember yourself.*

Tozi suppressed the desire to chuckle aloud, shaking her head. *You always know how to flatter, brother.* Her resolve strengthened. *If we are to do this, we must prepare completely.*

Kilmarii's enthusiasm was spilling into their shared mind stream.

The three of them turned to Kayko, surprised he had not announced his unbridled enthusiasm.

Kayko sat up with a serious face. *If we work together we can put all the ship animals to sleep, even the humans, but Jyukan and Tozi will need to put the entire camp to sleep. If that can be done, then we will not be detected. I have already put all the birds and canines to sleep.*

Tozi and Jyukan exchanged a glance, their thoughts entwining. Jyukan's mental tone sharpened, *It is too dangerous to leave the clan entirely vulnerable. If something were to happen, we will forever regret our indulgences.*

We limit our time, Jyukan said firmly, *no longer than the time it takes for the tide to shift. Agreed?*

To make this work, we will need to travel by dolphin, said Tozi, *but this will wake Maleia. She will see us through the dolphin.*

With Maleia wearing the earrings, she will be able to resist me, Kilmarii stated, knowing she had revealed the last of her secrets without regret. She continued, *We will need to travel by shark.*

The emotional mixture of fear and desire swirled in the other knowers. Kilmarii waited for them to settle on their decision.

Agreed, said Tozi.

Agreed, said Jyukan.

They all turned to Kayko, who finally spoke, *Select sharks you can trust. Agreed.*

The preparations were meticulous. The three powerful clan knowers sent a thunderous wave of mental energy through the animals aboard the ships and at the shore camp, guiding them into deeper sleep.

Kilmarii surprised Jyukan and Tozi with her ability to lull the entire camp into a deep sleep. It was both impressive and unsettling. She wielded powers that they did not fully understand, but tonight, they chose to trust her.

When they had finished, the clan's nocturnal guards, both human and animal, slipped into an unnatural calm, their minds lulled temporarily. Even the whales and other creatures of the ocean were sent in the opposite direction of the ships, and a path was opened below the surface to the island of the temple.

Kilmarii called four small hammerhead sharks to swim them to shore.

On the deck, the four knowers gathered, their hearts racing with the exhilaration of a new experience looming before them. The stars above

Lisa Newton

seemed brighter than before, the ocean below a dark expanse.

Jyukan surveyed the quiet camp one last time, his mind brushing over the edges of sleeping thoughts, ensuring no one stirred. The others did the same. The only fear was of Maleia awakening.

The four slipped silently down the rope ladders and into the water, their hearts pounding, their eyes watching Kilmarii as she grabbed onto her shark's dorsal fin. With trepidation, they did the same with their respective sharks.

The sharks began the swim to shore, their movements precise under the complete control of Kilmarii. The ocean's warmth enveloped them, a soft contrast to the night air. Unnerved by the juvenile hammerheads, the sharks traveled longer than any had expected.

Kilmarii led the way, her mental voice guiding the others, *We are close, just on the other side of these small islands.*

The rocks ahead looked different from the islands the Yutkis had been training on; their black surfaces were porous and sharp. Between them, the ocean churned over black sand beaches. The rhythmic swish of the sharks carried them closer to the hidden tide pool that led to the temple's cave entrance.

As they approached the entrance, the spiraled stone came into view. Its intricate pattern seemed to pulse faintly with an energy that resonated inside their minds. Tozi's breath halted for a moment, and

Kilmarii The Wayfinder

awe swept over her. *This place is an ancient vortex,* she whispered into their minds, *it is a womb.*

Without another word, they released their sharks and dove beneath the stone, entering the sacred cave. As the four swam through the water-filled opening of the cave, its beauty overwhelmed Tozi with wonder. For at that moment, she forgot her age, her fears, and her responsibilities. She felt the strength of her legs and shoulders return to her. She felt the silk of the water against her skin and the length of her hair floating free.

It was all there. The shimmering crystals, the sleeping sharks, the warm air bubbling up from the sands, and the water illuminating a light blue by the endless refraction of light off the crystal walls and ceiling, were exactly as Kilmarii had shown them.

As they swam, the four knowers exchanged a moment, acknowledging to one another the pure energy vibrating through them, their thoughts entangled in awe and reverence. A signal was given by Jyukan to rise to meet in the ceiling air fissure.

During high tide, the water must spurt out the vent, Jyukan observed.

They rotated their bodies, treading in the water, trying to observe all. Below them, sharks of all sizes and types floated, as if dead, in a dream-like state. Kayko attempted to connect to them, but got no response. Tozi and Jyukan also attempted to connect to the sharks, but got the same result.

Kilmarii explained in the mind stream, *The sharks are asleep in the air bubbles. They only wake when they are hungry and need to hunt.*

That is not comforting, Kilmarii. Kayko added, *We are easy meals, trapped inside this cave.*

The need for fresh air burned maliciously in their lungs. They swam back through the passage to the pool and surfaced to the night sky. The stars and moon welcomed them back, their hearts full and their minds alive with the beauty of what they had shared.

The four travelers glided with the sharks, silently through the warm waters of the bay, back to Maleia's ship. The night's adventure wrapped around them like a blanket.

Their ship loomed ahead, its dark silhouette rising against the horizon, and Kilmarii slowed the sharks with a gentle thought. The sharks circled beneath the hull, their movements synchronized as the four reached the ship's side. Kilmarii signaled silently, and one by one, they climbed the rope ladder, their wet bodies moving without sound.

On the deck, the world was still. Every animal remained in a deep, peaceful sleep, and the faint breathing of the crew drifted up from the sleeping quarters. They moved with careful precision, slipping into their respective places as though they had never left. Kilmarii focused her mind, releasing the humans from their deep slumber, while Tozi, Jyukan, and Kayko released the animals. Life resumed its normal rhythm, with no one the wiser.

But the four of them knew that they were not the same. The energy of the cave had seeped into their

Kilmarii The Wayfinder

very beings, altering them in ways that felt both profound and mysterious.

The next morning, Tozi sat in her small chamber, flexing her wrist slowly. She felt a youthful vitality coursing through her. The familiar ache that had plagued her for years was gone. She pressed her palms together, marveling at the fluidity and strength in her movements.

Jyukan stood near the doorway, his broad chest rising and falling steadily. He clenched his fists experimentally, marveling at the renewed strength in his arms and legs. His muscles felt invigorated, as though he had stepped back into the prime of his youth. As he rolled his shoulders back, he silently thanked the spirits of the water that granted this gift.

In her quiet corner, Kilmarii ran her fingers through her hair, which had rapidly grown long enough to cascade over her shoulders. She stared at the black strands in disbelief. Her body vibrated with energy, her senses heightened. She rolled over to look at Kayko, who stood nearby observing her. His frame was noticeably stronger, taller than hers for the first time.

But it was Kayko who noticed the connection between Jyukan, Tozi, and Kilmarii had deepened. Kayko rubbed the back of his neck, his thoughts contemplating the implications. He also felt mentally stronger, his thoughts more confident, and yet there was also a new awareness within him. He felt a twinge of something he could not name. Pride? Envy? Perhaps both. This adventure had changed something in all of them.

Kayko again looked at Kilmarii, and an undeniable truth settled in his mind. She was more powerful than he could ever hope to be, and she was beautiful. The realization did not bring jealousy but rather a profound respect and a quiet acceptance of their roles within the family.

Two mornings later, as the sun rose over the calm bay, the transformation in Jyukan and Tozi became unmistakable to the other clan members.

The sunlight reflected off the waves, casting a golden glow over the Esor and Yutki clans as they gathered their nets and spears for the day's fish hunt. High above, Maleia stood alone at the mast, her sharp eyes observing the preparations below.

Among the hunters, Jyukan moved with a newfound vigor. His broad shoulders squared, and his purposeful steps exuded strength. For nearly all of Kayko's life, Jyukan had left much of the physical labor to the younger clan members, opting instead to guide and instruct from the sidelines. But today was different. Today, he stepped onto one of the net vessels, ready to join the hunt alongside his clan. His presence sent a ripple of surprise through the group, and Kayko, watching from a distance, felt a swell of pride.

Beneath the surface, schools of fish shimmered like liquid silver, their movements synchronized as Jyukan reached out with his mind, projecting calm and guiding the school of fish toward the nets. The fish responded almost immediately, their chaotic patterns shifted as they aligned with the waiting nets.

Kayko watched his father intently, as Jyukan maneuvered the nets with the ease of someone half his age, his hands deftly tying knots and checking for weak points as he let the net glide between the two boats. Finally, the signal was given, Jyukan pulled in the net, his powerful arms and back straining. The younger people pulled behind him, struggling to match his pace.

Maleia watched in astonishment as Jyukan helped to pull a fully loaded net behind him towards shore. His face broke into a rare grin as they secured the catch.

"Aho!" he shouted, his voice beaming with satisfaction. The clan echoed loudly their approval, their respect for the elder growing with each display of skill.

Later that day, Tozi knelt beside an older woman who had twisted her ankle and had been brought to the medicine woman for treatment. The woman winced as Tozi gently pressed her fingers around the swollen joint. Her mind reached out to the woman, offering reassurance and comfort.

Tozi placed her hands over the injury, her palms radiating warmth as she focused her thoughts, pulling from the energy of the Temple of the Water, through her hands and into the injured ankle. Her mind sank into the woman's pain, finding the twisted ligaments and calming the inflammation. The woman stared in wonder as the warmth began to diminish the pain, replacing it with a tingling, cold sensation.

"It feels… better," she whispered, her hands enveloping the hands of Tozi, "I am grateful."

Tozi smiled, her weathered face glowing with quiet pride. "Good," she said, applying the medicine from the abalone shell, then tying a strip of soft leather around the ankle for support, "Rest here in my chamber for the night, and I will send water and food to you. In the morning. You will be able to stand and walk again."

Word of Tozi's healing abilities spread quickly, and soon a Yutki with a deep cut on her hand arrived at her threshold, followed directly by Lanakai, weary with an aching back. Each time, Tozi used her hands and medicines to heal harmoniously, channeling the energy that had rejuvenated her healer's spirit.

Jyukan's and Tozi's resurgence became a source of inspiration for the clan. The younger Yutki watched Jyukan with newfound respect, eager to learn from his strength and experience. Tozi's healing touch brought comfort to many, her presence a balm for both physical and emotional wounds.

Even Maleia, despite her sharp mind, could not piece together the puzzle of their sudden transformation, yet she was content that her clan thrived.

That evening, the knower meeting convened in the familiar circle below deck, the rhythmic sound

Kilmarii The Wayfinder

of waves creating the backdrop. Maleia sat at the center, her commanding presence radiating authority. Jyukan and Tozi took their places. Kayko sat beside his father, his posture stiff with anticipation.

Maleia's sharp voice cut through the quiet, "I have observed changes that demand explanation. Jyukan, Tozi, your renewed spirit energy has been noticed. What has brought this about?"

Tozi, Maleia's trusted friend and advisor, spoke first, "The healing of one's body and spirit is not always a mystery, Maleia. We have been living in a place of renewal and birth of new life. The ocean provides, and we have found new ways to align ourselves with its strength."

Maleia's eyes narrowed slightly. As Maleia spoke, Kilmarii listened intently from her own space, her mind tethered to Tozi and Jyukan's mind stream. She sensed the tension in the room and felt Kayko's unease.

Jyukan's voice entered the conversation, steady and paternal, "Maleia, the renewal you see is a blessing we have received. Our spirits and bodies have become more connected to the earth through the abundance of the water."

Maleia's mind remained shielded behind her gold scroll earrings, but the knowers caught her skepticism in her expression. Tozi, sensing the same, pressed on, "Healing is not just of the body but also of the mind. The clan benefits when its elders are strong."

Maleia's lips pressed into a thin line, "Yes, this is certain, and most welcomed by all."

Jyukan interjected confidently, "There is no coincidence, Maleia. The clan faces challenges. If we are stronger now, it is because we must be." He continued, "The clan depends on you as a leader who can guide them through uncertain waters and protect us from enemies. All this you are also doing."

Mentally, Kayko sent a hesitant, unsettled feeling to Kilmarii.

Kilmarii replied gently, *She always suspects more, but she cannot read minds like we can. Tozi and Jyukan are protecting us all.*

Maleia leaned back slightly, her piercing gaze sweeping over the circle, "Perhaps, but the clan thrives, and I will not question that it is the abundance of these waters that strengthens us."

When the meeting ended, the members began to disperse, but Jyukan lingered, catching Tozi's eye.

Jyukan sent a thought, his mind tinged with worry, *She knows something, does she not?*

Tozi responded cautiously, *She knows enough to be curious but not enough to act. We must maintain the balance.*

Kilmarii, still connected to the mental stream, sent her gratitude, *You protected me tonight. Thank you.*

Jyukan's response was measured by warmth, *We protect our own. Always.*

The waves continued their steady rhythm as the

Kilmarii The Wayfinder

clan prepared on the deck for the nightly meeting, but Maleia remained charged with unspoken tension. Tozi and Jyukan exchanged a final glance, their shared resolve unshaken. Whatever challenges lay ahead, they would face them together, as a family.

Chapter Nineteen

Discoveries & Instincts

The late afternoon sun glinted across the bay as Jyukan looked up, shading his eyes with a hand. The eagles were specks against the vast sky, flying south once again. Their loyalty to Maleia was unwavering, their purpose clear even when untethered from her mental commands. Jyukan felt the anxiety of anticipation as he watched them disappear toward the horizon, searching for signs of Ouray and the trading party.

He had been summoned to Ouray's ship by Maleia. The familiar scent of dried herbs and the many containers of things strewn about made him miss his brother even more. Maleia was bent over the large seal-skin map spread across the table, her gray hair pulled tightly back, the lines of her face etched in concentration. Her fingers traced a path along the map's surface.

"You are welcome to join me, Jyukan," she said without looking up, her voice heavy with unspoken concern. "We need to plan our return. There is much to discuss."

Jyukan stepped closer, his eyes scanning the map as Maleia straightened. Her gaze shifted to him, steady and piercing.

"Sedna is gone," she said bluntly. "She has joined a pod of whales heading out to sea. I called to her, but her pull to follow them was stronger than our bond."

Jyukan's jaw tightened; he felt like he had been punched in the gut, for he was unaware. He let out a slow breath, absorbing the weight of her words. Sedna's departure was not only a loss to their clan but a logistical blow to their plans to return home.

"Another whale cannot simply be harnessed without proper bonding," he said, his voice measured, "and even if we found one willing to pull a ship, crafting a harness without the resources would be impossible."

"Not impossible, but it would take too long, and we would arrive home when the ice is starting to form." Maleia looked up slowly at Jyukan. She was glad she wore her earrings so he could no longer know what was on her mind. Her attraction to him had grown since he returned to hunting with the

Yutkis, but it was immediately removed from her mind as she remembered the task at hand. She smiled when her eyes met Jyukan's, "As long as we are partners, we can win any battle."

Jyukan nodded, his expression grim. "We may have no choice but to leave one of the ships behind." He leaned over the map, his finger trailed along the marked routes back to their home waters. "Perhaps there is another way," he suggested, "we could dismantle the ship and divide its load among the remaining three. The materials could be repurposed to build a winter shelter or a storm structure, like the one we use in the highlands."

Maleia's forehead wrinkled, and her lips pressed together in contemplation. "Trading the ship with another clan could be an option as well," she offered, her tone more musing than dismissive, "Though the chances of finding another clan willing to barter something of that value would be difficult to find."

Before either could speak further, a ripple of awareness ran through Maleia's mind. Her posture stiffened, her sharp features softening into something unexpected: delight. The eagles had returned to her range, their images vivid and clear.

She turned to Jyukan, her eyes bright.

"They are here," she said, her voice tinged with rare joy. "Ouray, Jek, and the trading party. They have set up camp at the southern shore."

Almost immediately, Jyukan experienced a mental acknowledgment ripple through his own

Kilmarii The Wayfinder

mind. Tozi's presence bloomed alongside his, her relief as palpable as his own. The eagles' images spread quickly, touching every member of the clan. Soon, shouts of joy erupted across the ships and shore camp as the news was shared. People laughed, cheered, and called to one another, their collective excitement lighting up the bay in celebration.

Jyukan's smile faded, and unease simmered beneath his happiness at the trading parties' return. Among the many voices raised in celebration, two were noticeably absent: Kayko and Kilmarii. His mind reached out, but he encountered only silence.

Kilmarii, Kayko, answer me! Tozi said anxiously, her own attempts met with the same void.

Maleia's focus remained on the eagles' images, unaware of the concern threading through Jyukan and Tozi's private exchange. "We must prepare for their arrival immediately," she said joyfully to Jyukan.

Tozi had a premonition that Kilmarii and Kayko were at the Temple of the Water, and it was shielding them. She shared this with Jyukan.

Chapter Twenty

Quest of Comprehension

Unbeknownst to them, Kilmarii had slipped away, her plan carefully executed. Riding atop a sleek, familiar shark, she directed it toward the Temple of the Water. Her mind was singularly focused on her goal: collecting crystals from the sacred cave, a symbol of her connection to the place she once called home. She wanted to take them with her to the north, knowing it would likely be the last time she would ever be in a place she shared with her father.

When she arrived at the temple, the morning sunlight was rising on the horizon, and the rays of light majestically reached out to her. No one would miss her as she spent most of her time as a lone shark fighter, hanging onto a ladder or in the water.

Kilmarii The Wayfinder

As she expected, she arrived at the tide pool as the light was illuminating the spiral stone marking the entrance to the cave. Kilmarii dove into the warm, clear water and swam with purpose through the cave, her shark companion circling protectively nearby. Inside the cave, the crystals gleamed like trapped starlight, their edges sharp and perfect. She reached for one, trying to pry it free with her fingers and a wedge stone. The crystal resisted, its base deeply embedded in the rock of the cave.

The tide started its slow shift. The gentle rhythm of the waves transformed into a stronger pull. The water level rose, and soon, Kilmarii found herself trapped. The tide filled the cave, and she was forced upward into the diminishing air pocket at the base of the vent hole fissure.

She was forced to breathe in shallow gasps as waves splashed over her face. Each surge of water pushed her closer to panic, but she fought to stay calm, her strength waning, and her ability to maintain her shield decaying. And in her mind a familiar voice pierced through.

Kilmarii! Where are you? Kayko's mental voice was urgent, tinged with fear.

I am here, she replied weakly, her thoughts trembling with exhaustion. *The cave… I am trapped in the high tide,* she answered, her voice acknowledging desperation. *Promise me that you cannot come after me. The current is too strong.*

Kayko hesitated, his instincts screaming to act, but he knew she was correct.

I promise, he said reluctantly.

Unable to accept resignation, Kayko, instead of keeping his word, climbed past the temple's spiral-marked stone. He found the vent above the cave and tried to reach her through it, but the narrow opening allowed for little more than his voice to pass through, as he was intermittently met in the face with spray.

I cannot get to you this way, he said, frustration evident in his tone, *but I can wait here with you. You have to hold on until the tide changes.*

As the tide pulled out slowly, their minds stayed connected. From the dangerous churning inside the illuminated cave, Kilmarii shared her fear and determination, while Kayko offered her strength through his thoughts. They exchanged apologies for past hurts and promises for the future. And at one point, Kayko's mind feared a shark would wake and eat Kilmarii.

None of them are aware of me. I will not let them wake.

You are my family, Kayko earnestly told her, his mental voice as true as any man had ever spoken, *and I will never leave you behind.*

Kilmarii replied with sincere honesty, *I wasn't sure until this moment that I could trust in you.*

Why are you back in this cave? Kayko asked, deflecting the opportunity to make an oath pledge to Kilmarii that was welling up in his heart.

I just... I wanted something to connect me to where I came from and to my father, she confessed.

Kilmarii The Wayfinder

You do not need crystals from the Temple of Water for that, Kayko said, *you carry it all inside your blood and bones.*

Chapter Twenty-One

Declarations

The Yutkis and Esors worked steadily fishing and hunting in the tide pools, returning often to the ships with their catches. The clan moved efficiently through their routines, cleaning fish, sorting shellfish, and preparing everything for storage. Their chatter carried a blend of satisfaction and weariness, punctuated by laughter as they shared small victories of the day.

Jyukan exchanged the news with Tozi about Sedna leaving and worries about the ramifications. He said softly, his words meaning as much for himself as for her, "If they are in the Temple, they are safe for now. We will handle what comes when the time is right."

Tozi said she agreed, but the concern did not

leave her. Regardless, they both turned their attention back to Ouray and the preparations ahead.

As the jubilant cries of the clan continued to reverberate in echoes across the bay, Tozi and Jyukan found their minds growing heavy with worry. The absence of Kayko and Kilmarii from the shared mental stream hung as a dark shadow over them.

In the quiet of the lower deck of Maleia's ship, Tozi closed her eyes and let her mind extend outward. She sifted through the currents of thought and emotion among the fish and animals in her range, seeking any sign of the two.

Jyukan stood at the rail of Ouray's ship, his broad shoulders tense, his mind casting further out into the waters, probing deeper into the creatures that inhabited the bay, trying to locate his children. His mental reach grew sharper as he focused on the dolphins, the seabirds, even the elusive rays gliding along the ocean floor. Yet the results were the same: blank spaces where there should be fragments of the young knowers' movements or intentions.

Have they done this intentionally?

No, Tozi's face hardened as concern gave way to anger. *They have returned to the Temple of the Water,* she stated with certainty. *Where else could they be, if not in the only place they know we cannot track them?* Tozi exhaled sharply, her hands gripped the necklace beneath her tunic. *We gave them trust. We taught them shielding, believing they would use it wisely. And now they have turned it against us.*

For a moment, their shared anger filled the space between them. Tozi's mind flashed with memories of long nights spent guiding Kilmarii through lessons in shielding and Kayko's eagerness to prove himself a strong partner. Now those memories felt tarnished by the sting of betrayal.

What do we do, Tozi asked, *if they are at the temple? We cannot swim out and bring them back without the clan knowing where we are going. We will have to explain how we put the clan in jeopardy.*

We wait, Jyukan said after a long pause, though his tone was laced with more worry than frustration. *They will return if they have just gone on a foolish adventure. They know they cannot stay hidden forever.*

And when they do?

They will answer for this, Jyukan replied, his voice unyielding. *This is more than disobedience. It is reckless and selfish, and they must understand the gravity of their actions.*

Tozi's mind churned with conflicting emotions. Anger, yes, but also a gnawing fear for the children who had taken such a dangerous path. She wondered if Jyukan felt the same fear beneath his stern exterior.

They are still children, Tozi said softly, almost to herself.

They are powerful and skilled clan knowers, Jyukan replied firmly, *and they must be responsible to the standards of what that means.*

Kilmarii The Wayfinder

Meanwhile, the sun lowered over the vast stretch of southern shore as Ouray shifted uncomfortably on Jek's broad back. His muscles ached from the extended journey, and even Jek seemed slower than usual, his powerful movements deliberate as they approached the camp. Ouray's mind extended outward, scanning the returning eagles long before they came into view. Their sharp, focused thoughts provided a glimpse of the path ahead, carrying images of the trading party's progress and the growing activity among the clans.

The southern shore bustled with life as another clan's camp came into view. Tents stood steady against the breeze, and the scent of smoked fish and roasted birds wafted through the air. Ouray's party exchanged polite greetings and began making trade, an exchange that ensured alliances without binding obligations. Once the trades concluded, the group moved westward to make camp, where their stored vessels awaited.

By dusk, the camp had taken shape. Firelight danced over the faces of the traders as they set up shelters and secured provisions. The rhythmic lapping of waves mingled with the snorts and clawing sounds of Ouray's surprise. The Yutkis among the group sat softening the dolphin harnesses for use in transporting the vessels to the whale ships. Ouray leaned closely over the map, mentally calculating the time it would take for the ships to anchor off their shore once the eagles reached Maleia and Jyukan. He estimated the fleet would arrive by the following night.

Ouray's mind sharpened, reaching out toward the clan members aboard the arriving ships. He swiftly scanned for Jyukan, Tozi, or even Kayko. At first, he focused on the immediate needs of the fleet, gathering details of their journey and the clans' preparations for departure. But soon, disjointed fragments of thought caught his attention, images and emotions that did not align with routine events.

Ouray's face grew still as he absorbed the shared memories of Jyukan, Tozi, and others. The Temple of the Water adventure unfolded in vivid flashes: the crystalline caves, the hammerhead sharks, and the charged energy that left Jyukan and Tozi revitalized.

His amazement was accompanied by the pang of jealousy, as such an adventure had occurred without him. The potential of the temple's water to strengthen the body and mind intrigued him deeply. What might it do for someone like him?

But the intrigue quickly gave way to a rising wave of alarm. As his mind swept further, seeking the young knowers, he realized there was nothing. Kayko and Kilmarii were not there. His siblings' thoughts revealed the length of time the children had been silent—two tides, perhaps more.

Ouray's jaw clenched down, and with urgency, his mental reach fully expanded. He skimmed the edges of the camp, probed the waters nearby, and brushed against the faint minds of dolphin pods swimming around the bay. Still, there was no trace

Kilmarii The Wayfinder

of Kayko or Kilmarii. His mind pressed further, combing the fragments left in the thoughts of others, piecing together the timeline.

"They have gone to the temple again," he muttered under his breath, his voice low and troubled. "Reckless, foolish children."

Jek shifted beneath him, sensing the tension in his rider's thoughts. Ouray straightened, forcing his body to calm even as his mind churned. *If the children have returned to the temple, their survival depends on their ability to work together to survive. The danger is undeniable. Without clear communication, there is no way to know if they have been injured, trapped, or worse.*

Chapter Twenty-Two

Promises

F inally, the tide receded enough for Kayko to enter the cave safely. He swam through the channel, his heart pounding as he spotted Kilmarii, battered and barely conscious, clutching a cluster of purple crystals. Her fingers were scraped raw, and her limbs were weak, but she was alive.

Kilmarii, he whispered in their mind stream, his relief overwhelming as he pulled her close, *do not let the sharks eat us.*

Kilmarii smiled, *I promise.*

Kilmarii The Wayfinder

Chapter Twenty-Three

Under Tozi's Protection

As the camp settled for the night, Ouray opened the conversation between himself and his siblings, *They are young, but if they have returned to the temple, they must have had a reason.*

Ouray, what do you sense of them? Tozi asked.

Ouray shook his head, *Nothing. They are shielding or they are too far. It is deliberate— whether for safety or secrecy, I cannot say. But it is time to go get them.*

We wait for dawn, Jyukan declared. *If there is no sign of them, I will go myself.*

For a long moment, silence stretched between them, heavy with unspoken fears. Tozi spoke with the authority of her age and position over her siblings, *No, we will go to them now.*

Ouray stepped to the edge of the camp, his mind reaching once more into the vast expanse of water and sky. He was physically too far to be of assistance. Somewhere, the children were out there, silent, shielded, and beyond his reach. The weight of their absence pressed against him like the pull of the tide. He let out a slow breath, his thoughts a silent plea for their safety as the night deepened around him.

Chapter Twenty-Four

Pride

Together, Kayko and Kilmarii navigated the retreating currents and emerged into the pool. As they surfaced, gasping for air, they found themselves under the watchful eyes of Malka, Lanikai, and Kayloni standing on the rocks above. Their expressions were unreadable in the moonlight, their silence heavy with judgment.

Kayko stammered, "I—" but Kilmarii's body slumped against him, unconscious.

While Lanikai and Kayloni readied Kilmarii to ride by dolphin power back to the ship, Malka instructed Kayko to take her into the cave.

Malka marveled at first at the beauty of the cave, but surfaced immediately upon seeing the multitudes of sharks suspended above the bubbling sand. She swam quickly, returning through the water-filled cave tunnel into the tide pool.

Kayko read Malka's thoughts and did not interfere when she explained what she saw in the cave to her sisters, "She came to this cave to kill sharks. There are many sharks of all sizes floating dead at the bottom of the cave."

"Mother will be proud of her... grateful towards her now," Malka confidently pronounced.

"Yes, I agree," Kayloni replied.

And in the mind-stream, Kayko asked Tozi, *Did you have to send them?*

Be grateful I did not send Maleia, herself, Tozi responded.

Chapter Twenty-Five

Empathy

The Yutkis and Esors left behind their work as the sun sank lower, painting the bay in golden hues, shooting between stratus clouds. Another day of fruitful fishing and hunting in the tide pools had concluded. They returned to the ships with their catches.

The clan moved efficiently through their routines, cleaning fish, sorting shellfish, and preparing everything for storage. Their chatter carried a blend of satisfaction and weariness, punctuated by laughter as they shared small victories of the day. They paused only briefly for an evening meal before gathering for the nightly clan meeting.

The clan members gathered at night, especially

eager to hear if the rumors were true. Maleia stood tall in the center. She raised her hand, signaling for silence.

"Our trading party has returned," she began, her voice steady and clear.

Relief and excitement coursed through the group, soft murmurs quickly quieted to hear more.

"Ouray and his team have set up camp at the southern shore. Tomorrow morning, three ships will sail to retrieve the trade goods and our people."

The clan murmured their approval, nodding and exchanging glances. Maleia let the moment settle before continuing.

"There is also news of loss," she said, her tone heavier. "Sedna, our loyal whale, has left the bay. She was called by a pod and could not resist the pull. Though I called to her, her bond with them was stronger."

A wave of sadness washed over the clan, heads bowing in quiet respect for Sedna's departure.

"We must address the challenges this creates," Maleia continued, her voice firm. "Without Sedna, we will not be able to return with all four ships. Jyukan and I agree that we must consult Ouray and the elders to determine the best course of action."

Jyukan stepped forward, his broad shoulders squared, his voice resolute, "We will adapt, as we always have. Tomorrow, while the ships retrieve the trade goods and our people, we will begin preparing for the journey home."

Maleia nodded at Jyukan before allowing a

Kilmarii The Wayfinder

small smile to soften her expression. She raised her arms wide.

"And there is cause for celebration as well," she announced. "Kilmarii has returned from a successful shark hunt in a cave, where she has killed many large sharks, thus proving her worth and strength!"

The clan reacted with enthusiasm, clapping and cheering. Pride exuded from the minds of even those who once doubted Kilmarii, and they cheered in approval. Heads turned to look for Kilmarii, and did not find her.

"We will honor Sedna's memory and prepare ourselves for what lies ahead," Maleia said. "Now, let us call our whales home."

Maleia stepped to the edge of the ship, the ocean breeze lifting strands of her hair. Closing her eyes, she raised her arms, her voice resonating with a powerful, melodic tone that seemed to vibrate through the air. The clan joined in, their voices blending with hers in a low, reverberating chant. Feet stomped against the wooden decks, creating a steady rhythm that mimicked the heartbeat of the ocean.

The sound carried across the water, growing louder, more unified. Then, from the depths of the ocean, they saw them—Yachai, Kaiyah, her calf, and Wanahi. The whales leaped from the sea, their massive bodies glistening in the moonlight, sending cascades of water into the air as they crashed back down. The clan erupted in cheers, their minds reaching out to the whales with waves of welcome and gratitude.

Tears streaked down the cheeks of many clan members, a shared elation filled the air. For a moment, all doubts and fears faded, replaced by the profound bond between humans and whales. The harnesses would wait until morning; at that moment, the clan could only celebrate.

Small groups gathered on the decks, sharing food, stories, and laughter. The atmosphere was light, joyful, and deeply connected.

As the night grew calmer, Maleia called for a knower meeting, as there had not been time for one prior to the clan meeting.

The knowers gathered, their minds connected to one another as the sound of waves filtered through the stillness. Maleia's presence was different tonight, she was not as commanding as she usually was when addressing them.

"We will leave early tomorrow," Maleia stated. "Jyukan, Tozi, and I will go to the camp to meet Ouray. But this time, things will be different."

Jyukan raised an eyebrow, "Different how, Maleia?"

Maleia's expression shifted into a warmth seldom seen in her, "We will bring our children with us. It is time that they join in the leadership of the clan."

Surprise rippled through the knowers, none more so than Kayko, but Tozi spoke first, her voice tinged with hesitation, "Kilmarii? Are you certain?"

Kilmarii The Wayfinder

"I am certain," Maleia replied, her tone brooking no argument. "Kilmarii has proven her worth. She deserves to be part of these discussions, to learn and contribute. As will my children."

Jyukan nodded slowly, though his thoughts were cautious, "And Kayko?"

Maleia allowed a small smile, "Yes, of course. These meetings must include all of us, for the challenges ahead require unity and shared strength."

A long pause lingered, as all remained silent, digesting the great change that had been initiated by Maleia.

"We move forward together," Maleia concluded, her voice resonating in the mental stream. "Rest tonight. Tomorrow begins a new chapter for us all."

Chapter Twenty-Six

Acceptance

When Kilmarii awakened, she was warm, clean, and cocooned in the safety of her family. Jyukan's strong arms cradled her protectively, his steady breathing a soothing rhythm in the quiet of the night. She did not need to open her eyes to know Tozi was nearby, and she slipped back into a deep sleep.

Sooner than she would have liked, Kayko whispered in Esor, "The last one up cleans the chamber pots."

Before her eyes fluttered open, a bright smile spread across her face. *Welcome back, Ouray!* she mentally called out joyfully.

Kilmarii opened her eyes, and the room filled with quiet laughter and murmured relief. Tozi's

Kilmarii The Wayfinder

worried face filled her entire vision. Though her body ached and her spirit was weary, Kilmarii felt the unshakable strength of her family around her, their love always ready to shield against the storms to come.

She had the strength to shed her past and to begin a new life as a daughter in a new family. Her spirit soared higher and farther than her mind could reach, up into the heavens and down into the depths of the sea.

Chapter Twenty-Seven

Threads Unraveling

By the time Kilmarii and Kayko reached the Yutki meal area, Tesi and the others were in the water harnessing the whales. The ship fires were out, and every member of the clan was busy with preparations.

In the distance, Kilmarii saw Ouray's ship's sails being lowered and tied down, after which the anchors would soon be set. Directly behind the ship was the shoreline of tide pools where they had trained, and, beyond that, the Temple of the Water.

She wasn't sure if it was her newly developed security or a calling from the sacred ways of her clan, ignited by her time inside the Temple of the Water, but Kilmarii felt the call to resume her

Kilmarii The Wayfinder

temple worship practice.

Kilmarii closed her eyes; the sun warmed her skin. She began to breathe slowly in and out of her nose. Her mind's eye created a channel of rotating light between her forehead and the Sun. She reached out her right palm in the direction of the Temple of the Water, and turned her left palm to the depths of the sea.

Her spirit was transported forward into a pure white void from which the image of a black jaguar carrying a cub in her mouth came into focus. Her subconscious forced her to inhale sharply, and the connection was severed. The warmth of hands enveloped hers. She turned her head and opened her eyes to find Kayko's face nearly touching hers.

"Tozi is calling us," Kayko said aloud.

He finished his message mentally, *She wants us to take a vessel to Ouray's ship to retrieve medicines for her to bring to Ouray's camp before the whales move.*

Chapter Twenty-Eight

Resolve

When three ships crested the horizon ahead of schedule, Ouray's brow furrowed. He scanned the decks as they approached, expecting to see familiar faces.

The clan members on the shore called out to the ships and the clan on board began the stop chant. Quickly vessels were lowered down the sides of the ships, followed closely behind by diving Yutkis ready to harness dolphins. Among them were Kayko and Jyukan.

Kilmarii, still recovering from her wounds from the cave walls was forbidden to be in the water for fear her blood would attract the sharks. She and Tozi lowered themselves down a rope ladder and into one of the first vessels headed to the shore camp. They had been mentally summoned to

Kilmarii The Wayfinder

Ouray's tent.

Maleia, Malka, Lanikai, and Kayloni soon joined them on the same mission, in the same vessel. Maleia took command of the dolphins, and they soon found themselves in the waves lapping gently on the sandy shoreline of the camp. The air buzzed with activity as the clan formed lines to pass the supplies into the vessels.

Ouray sat near a makeshift table covered with maps and notes, his broad shoulders cast in shadow by the light of the rising sun. His deep brown eyes met Kilmarii's as she approached, and a deep laugh rose out of his belly. He was already aware of all that had transpired, thanks to the mental connection he shared with his knower family.

"Ouray," Kilmarii greeted him, her voice respectful, "I am full of joy to see you and learn details of your trade journey."

Ouray, where is your armadillo? Kayko inquired mentally.

Ouray gestured his head toward the clan delegation approaching.

He looked at Kayko, and responded in kind, *Ahhh... playing with the baby armadillos, I suppose.*

Is this true? Kayko made it evident that Ouray and he were engaged in a knower conversation, *Where are they?*

Kayko touched Kilmarii's shoulder, smiled playfully, and ran in the direction of Jek.

"Kilmarii," Ouray spoke warmly. "You have

been busy."

Kilmarii continued to speak aloud, to keep her abilities a secret, "I imagine you have many questions, my favorite uncle."

"More than I can count," Ouray said with a chuckle, "but they can wait. First, we must solve the problem of my ship."

Maleia dismissed her daughters to assist with the loading of the supplies.

The knower family exchanged glances as their mental conversation started to overlap with the spoken one.

"Ouray," Tozi interjected, her tone firm but kind, "you must tell us your stories on the journey home. They will keep us entertained for many nights."

"Agreed," Jyukan added with a nod, "but first, the whale."

Kilmarii stepped forward, her confidence solid. "I have an idea," she offered confidently and clearly. "What about a whale shark?"

Ouray raised an eyebrow, intrigued, "A whale shark? Explain."

Kilmarii described the massive creature, her hands moving as she spoke, "It looks like a whale and eats like a whale, but it swims much slower than a whale. It is gentle and feeds only on plankton and small creatures floating in the water. It could pull your ship, though the journey north would take longer."

Maleia stood up from her quiet perch. She had

listened long enough and knew more was said between the knowers that she was not privileged to know.

Ouray nodded thoughtfully, but before he could respond, Maleia's voice cut through the mental exchange.

"A shark?" she asked sharply, her tone skeptical. She walked into the center of the meeting circle, her dark eyes narrowed. "You would suggest a predator to guide one of our ships?"

"It is not like other sharks," Kilmarii insisted, her voice firm and respectful. "It is as peaceful as Yachai. It eats the same as our whales."

Maleia exchanged a look with Jyukan, her expression hard, "The clan will never agree. Fear of sharks runs too deep. The risk is too great."

"Maleia," Kilmarii turned her back to Jyukan, and appealed to Maleia directly, "I do not know if I have the power to control one or even to call one to us, but if I am able to do this, will you allow me to present this idea to the whales and the clan leadership?"

Ouray turned to Maleia and respectfully indicated his approval. "It is worth discussing."

At the nightly clan meeting, with Maleia, Jyukan, and the rest of the leadership standing behind her, Kilmarii stood, her shoulders squared, her voice steady, as she addressed concerns.

"A whale shark is not a predator to fear," she explained. "It will not harm the whales or the clan. It eats only the smallest creatures in the ocean, filtering plankton through its massive mouth. It is slow and steady, and I can guide it safely."

The clan elders listened and murmured among themselves. And when asked if Yachai, Kaiyah, and Wanahi had agreed to swim with a shark, Kilmarii had to admit that the whales rejected the idea outright, unwilling to share their journey with even a gentle shark.

Maleia's sharp tone echoed their decision. "The clan fears sharks, and for good reason. We will not rely on one to guide us home."

Ouray spoke next, his voice calm and striving to persuade, "Kilmarii's plan could work. If Kilmarii stays with me, I can assist her in maintaining control over the whale shark. Because it is slower than our whales, I propose this plan. If the whale shark brings my ship part of the way north, it could be released before entering our waters. Yachai could then return to bring us the rest of the way."

Maleia and Jyukan exchanged a long look before nodding.

"Minimal supplies and crew," Maleia stated firmly. "No risks to the rest of the clan."

"I will agree to it." Jyukan added, "Kilmarii must stay with the ship to guide the whale shark. Kayko, however, will remain with me."

Kayko bristled but remained silent, his frustration echoing in the minds of Tozi and Jyukan.

This is unfair, he thought, all his emotions spilling into Kilmarii's awareness.

Kilmarii The Wayfinder

Chapter Twenty-Nine

Summoning a Whale Shark

The moonlight cast silver, wavy lines streaked on top of the dark water as Kilmarii walked toward Ouray's shelter. While most of the clan had found sleep, Kilmarii had not. Her heart felt heavy, weighed down by the uncertainty of what lay ahead, so she sought out the one person she felt might hold sound advice to guide her next move.

However, when she arrived, she found Ouray had a guest. He and Maleia were seated near a small wooden table, deep in conversation. They turned their heads as she approached, both their expressions welcoming her presence.

"I need help," Kilmarii said softly, her voice trembling despite her effort to sound confident. "I do not know if I can summon the whale shark."

Maleia's sharp eyes studied her, and after a moment of silence, she nodded. "Your fear is not weakness. Come closer, child," Maleia said, gesturing for her to sit. "I can guide you, but first, I wish to share something of my own."

Ouray leaned back, his expression encouraging, *Listen with wisdom, Kilmarii.*

Kilmarii hesitated, her gaze flicking between them, but then she nodded and sat.

Maleia reached out for Kilmarii's hand and grasped it, her voice dropping into a tone both solemn and reflective, "I know what you have endured, Kilmarii. Ouray has told me some, and I can see much in your actions. You are a substitute daughter, cast onto the sea to survive or die, much like I was.

Maleia's voice grew heavier, laced with an old grief, "When I was a child, I was of the common people, a girl of promise who could hunt and fish as well as any warrior, man or woman. My people valued my skills, but fate had other plans.

"One day, I was taken by the high temple family, chosen to replace their priestess daughter, who had failed them. I was made to take her place, taught to act as her, speak as her, and in every way, become someone I was not. It was a secret they guarded fiercely. The unwanted daughter, hidden away, took my place among the common warriors. I never saw my family again."

Kilmarii listened in stunned silence, her breath

catching as Maleia's words echoed in her mind. Through the mental link, Tozi and Jyukan listened as well, their emotions tinged with sorrow and empathy, for they had been holding this secret for Maleia for some time.

"I often wonder," Maleia continued, her voice softening, "how would my stolen life have been? Did that hidden daughter succeed as a warrior? Did my family thrive without me? These questions remain unanswered.

"And yet, I see you, Kilmarii, and I see myself. You are not a mind knower as the priestess families are, but you are of a warrior's blood. You have the strength to hunt, to control the sharks, to summon animals. It is a gift born of your lineage, as mine was controlled from a great distance."

Kilmarii started to feel the dizziness of succumbing to stress; her hands gripped the edge of the table. She fought the urge to reveal the truth, that she was an unwanted priestess daughter, cast away by her people.

Do not reveal yourself, Tozi sent out to her.

Maleia reached up and took hold of Kilmarii's face with both hands, "You are my sister in spirit, Kilmarii. A sister warrior of the same clan. We share blood and bone. And I will teach you what you need to know."

Kilmarii blinked back tears, nodding silently as Maleia led her toward the water's edge. The moonlight traveled along the surface, skipping atop the waves and coloring the fine sand in hues of

Kilmarii The Wayfinder

silver. The air hummed with the rhythmic sound of the tide.

"Close your eyes," Maleia instructed, her voice low and steady. "Feel the energy of the ocean. Let your mind extend beyond yourself. Seek the creature you need. It is out there, waiting."

Kilmarii inhaled deeply, closed her eyes as Maleia instructed. Her mind stretched across the water like the tide, brushing against the thoughts and movements of the ocean's life. She felt Maleia's body behind her, matching her own in form.

Maleia intertwined their fingers and then raised their arms outstretched wide. Schools of fish darted away from their mental touch. The far-off echoes of whales filled her awareness, but Kilmarii pushed past them, seeking something larger, slower, more serene.

Maleia watched her intently; then, in a soft, resonant tone, she began to hum—a deep, melodic sound that carried across the waves. Kilmarii felt the vibration in her chest, her voice rising to join it. Together, their harmony wove together through the night, a call that reached far into the depths of the sea.

Time stretched, the call hanging in the air. Kilmarii's mind brushed against the emptiness of the open ocean, but she refused to let doubt take root. She focused harder, her spirit searching, reaching deeper, farther.

And then, faintly, she felt it. A massive

presence, gentle yet immense, gliding through the water. Its mind was seeking her, its thoughts simple and unthreatened. A whale shark.

Kilmarii's connection sharpened. She pulled the creature closer with her thoughts, her mental touch filled with respect and purpose. Maleia's voice harmonized with hers, amplifying the call.

Finally, from beneath the surface, the enormous shark spoke out to Kilmarii. Kilmarii had summoned her whale shark.

The outline of Kilmarii and Maleia united was illuminated by the moonlight. Throughout the night, Maleia assisted Kilmarii in performing the bonding ritual with the whale shark.

"It is here, in the deeper water, not far from Ouray's ship," Kilmarii whispered, her voice trembling with awe.

Maleia shared in the triumph of the summoning, her tone approving, "You have summoned it. Now, it will be your bond to nurture. This is your path, sister warrior….AHO!" Maleia's praise filled the void in the silence of camp, stirring curiosity amongst the clan within hearing range.

Kilmarii stepped into the water, her heart racing as she reached out to the whale shark. The gentle rhythm of the waves carried Kilmarii's voice as she stood at the water's edge, her focus fixed on the great creature gliding beneath the surface. The whale shark, massive and serene, responded to her mental touch with a calm acceptance that surprised even Kilmarii. Its slow movements stirred the water, a shadow of quiet power against the moonlit sea.

"It is here," Kilmarii repeated, her voice full of youthful joy, but despite the awe she felt, she added, "It is feeding nearby, in deeper water, and does not wish to come closer."

Through the extension of her hand, her mind traveled a vast distance. The whale shark sent back to her a memory of it being released from a tide pool into the ocean by human hands.

Maleia stepped away, releasing her hold of Kilmarii. She kept her gaze sharp and assessed as she watched Kilmarii establish a true connection with her whale shark.

"You have done well to summon it, but the work has only just begun. This whale shark must understand its role, and that understanding must come from you."

The large creature lingered just beneath the surface. Kilmarii sent it waves of gratitude and reassurance. She felt the whale shark's acceptance wash over her.

Kilmarii nodded, her mind already reaching back to the whale shark, sending waves of calm encouragement. She sensed its curiosity, its trust bond beginning to form. The connection felt natural, effortless, as she realized she had known how to do this all her life.

Maleia folded her arms, her expression unreadable. "Then it is time to prepare. The ship must sail to deeper water before the harness can be fitted. And the harness itself must be made."

Instinctively, Ouray knew Maleia was setting him to this task. He nodded in agreement, "We will need precise measurements of the whale shark before the harness can be crafted. But the leather cords must be prepared now. There will be no time to waste once the creature is ready."

Maleia turned on her heel sharply, her voice rang with authority as she began issuing orders, "Pare, come here!"

Pare, a steady and resourceful member of the clan, hurried to Maleia's side.

"Yes, I am here. How may I be of service?" she asked, her tone eager and attentive.

"You are to oversee the preparation of the leather cords for the whale shark harness," Maleia said. "Ensure that there is enough material, and that the cords are braided strongly enough to hold. Work through the day and night until it is done."

Pare acknowledged the orders quickly, "It will be done."

Ouray turned suddenly pale; he heard a child within Pare.

Kilmarii noticed Ouray's heart started to beat harder.

Are you unwell, Ouray? Kilmarii inquired.

I am very well, Kilmarii. I am grateful that the whale shark has been successfully summoned. Please continue to focus on your task.

The clan continued to move with purpose and urgency. Hunters and fishers worked to bring in

Kilmarii The Wayfinder

leather from stored reserves, while others gathered tools for braiding and stitching. The sound of activity filled the air—voices calling out instructions, the soft thud of tools, and the rhythmic tugging of leather cords being stretched.

From their post atop the mast, Maleia and Jyukan had a heartfelt conversation, confirming that all was in balance and as it should be. For the first time, Jyukan wished Maleia had the power to know his mind.

Throughout the night and into the morning hours, Kilmarii remained by the water's edge, her mind linked to the whale shark. She sensed its steady movements below, its slow and deliberate feeding. It was oblivious to the flurry of activity preparing for it to join the clan.

Tozi arrived, carrying a bowl of water and sweet yellow fruit. "You need nourishment, my dear one."

For a long time, Tozi watched Kilmarii, choosing to speak her words aloud. "You have been given a gift by Ouray," she said quietly, "and a gift from Maleia. Do not waste it feeling unworthy of either." She continued her advice, "The whale shark must follow you because it trusts you. That trust is fragile. Do not lose it."

"I will not," Kilmarii promised with all earnestness.

Ouray arrived next to Kilmarii, atop of Jek, his expression thoughtful. "When we move the ship to deeper water, you will need to guide the whale shark alongside us. It must understand its purpose, or it will refuse the harness."

"I will guide it," Kilmarii said confidently. "It will stay with us."

As the clan worked through the day and night to prepare for the journey home, so too did Kilmarii. She had not rested, and as a result, Kilmarii felt the bond with the whale shark had deepened so that she could read its thoughts.

Its thoughts were simple, its emotions pure.

She sent waves of reassurance, promising it would not be harmed, that it would have purpose and respect among her people.

The second day rose and fell, and as the moon began to sink lower on the horizon, its pale light replaced by the faint glow of dawn, the braided cords had been completed and were coiled up under Pare's supervision.

Chapter Thirty

Sailing Home

It was the last evening meeting in the nursery bay; clan members, heavy from exhaustion, sat awaiting the updates from Maleia. The warm glow of the evening sun cast long rays of pink and orange behind the radiant Maleia. The air was thick with anticipation, the day's events still fresh in everyone's minds.

Maleia stood at the center, her posture commanding as always, her voice steady as she started to speak, "Today, we have finalized preparations for our three ships to journey home. The whales are ready, our supply rooms are spilling over, ready to return home. But there is more to discuss—important events that affect us all."

Her sharp eyes scanned the group, lingering

briefly on Kilmarii, Tozi, and Jyukan before she continued, "As you all know, Sedna has left us. She has joined a pod that called her away from our bay. While this is a loss, it is also a reminder of the bonds we share with these creatures. Sedna's spirit remains with the clan, but her strength will no longer pull one of our ships."

A low murmur grew throughout the group, some nodding solemnly.

"This brings me to an unusual celebration," Maleia said, her voice cutting through the chatter. "Kilmarii has summoned a whale shark to replace Sedna. Jyukan and I have agreed to let her attempt to guide the whale shark to pull Ouray's ship as far north as it is willing, and from there, Yachai will bring the ship the rest of the way."

The unsettled clan members grew louder, and Maleia held up a hand for silence, "I understand your concerns. Sharks have long been our enemies. But this is no ordinary shark. It is a peaceful creature, more whale than predator. Kilmarii assures us she can control it, and I have chosen to trust her."

Her words hung in the air, which was laden with unspoken tension. The clan members exchanged glances, struggling through their guarded thoughts and emotions that were swirling like the tide.

Jyukan stepped forward, his voice confident, "This decision was not made lightly. Kilmarii's abilities are unique, and we must consider every option to ensure our safe return. If we work together, we can overcome the challenges ahead."

Tozi stepped forward, alongside her brother, adding her voice, softer but no less impactful, "We are a clan that survives by adapting. This is no different. Trust in our bond and in the wisdom that has brought us this far."

The clan fell silent, their collective unease slowly ebbing under the weight of the elders' words.

Maleia looked out at the gathered clan, her voice carrying loudly, "Trust in the path before us and prepare for the task ahead."

The meeting concluded with subdued agreement that the whale shark would be used to guide Ouray's ship home. The clan dispersed to their ships, while Kilmarii lingered for a moment, her mind heavy with the weight of what was to come.

Chapter Thirty-One

Ouray's Ship

The ship decks were a whirlwind of activity as the ship's holds were restructured to properly supply Ouray's ship. Kayko darted among the bustling clan members, but his attention was fixated on the two young armadillos Ouray had brought back.

"These two are amazing!" Kayko exclaimed, crouching to observe the small creatures. One was a sturdy male, with a shell mottled in shades of grey and brown, and the other was a sleek female with lighter, almost golden hues.

They sniffed cautiously at Kayko, their sharp claws scratching against the walls of the wooden pen they had been placed in for transport to Ouray's ship.

Kilmarii The Wayfinder

"They'll do more than amaze you, Kayko," Ouray said, his voice carried over the clamor. "The male and female will grow strong enough to help the Nek with building and hauling. If they breed, even better. We need more animals like them."

Kayko grinned, extending a hand to the male armadillo. "What do you call them?"

Ouray smirked, "They are yours to name."

Kayko's eyes lit up, and he mentally reached toward the creatures. The male nudged his hand, and Kayko laughed, "I'll think of something fitting."

Kilmarii glanced at the two armadillos now resting in a shaded corner of the deck. She gave them a small smile before turning her attention back to the task of fitting the harness to the whale shark.

What do we call your whale shark? Kayko asked.

The name appeared in her mind, but stuck in her mouth, "*Bbbaaalkii*".

Balkii—the name resurfaced in Kilmarii's mind like a whispered secret. She had kept the story to herself, the name of the hairless black dog she had left behind, a loyal companion from another life. The enormous whale shark swimming below her ship sparked this memory to life, its dark grey skin with white spots gliding effortlessly through the water.

Balkii, the whale shark, was enormous, the length of Ouray's ship, its shadow a shifting patchwork of dots beneath the calm surface.

Kilmarii leaned over the rail, her thoughts reaching out to the gentle giant. Balkii responded with a pulse of curiosity and trust that settled Kilmarii's nerves.

"Is it close enough?" Kayko asked aloud, his tone was a mix of practicality and encouragement as he stepped up beside her.

"Yes," Kilmarii replied softly, "it followed us and is swimming under us."

Kayko leaned over to view it for himself, *I have never seen a whale that big!*

The bustling activity of the ship slowed as the crew prepared for a critical moment: fitting the harness to Balkii, the whale shark. The sun was high, casting blinding reflections on the waves.

Pare approached Kilmarii with a leather harness in hand, shaking her head slightly, "The harness is coming along, but it requires a fit test. We need to have this ready before the harness makers leave for home."

Kilmarii understood the ramifications. "Balkii is close, I will ask Kayko to help me."

Kayko crouched, running his hands over the sturdy harness. "This looks strong, but we need to be sure it fits perfectly."

Pare handed Kilmarii one end of the harness, the leather warm from the sun, "Let us do this carefully. We cannot afford mistakes."

Together, they lowered a small vessel into the water. Kilmarii steadied herself on the edge, the harness coiled neatly at her feet. Kayko joined her,

Kilmarii The Wayfinder

his usual playful demeanor replaced by fierce determination.

As they paddled out toward Balkii, the enormous whale shark slowly swam closer. Its spotted body was mesmerizing beneath the crystal-clear water. Kilmarii closed her eyes briefly, sending a message of reassurance to the gentle creature. Balkii responded by slowing to a near stop.

Kayko leaned over the side of the boat. *He trusts you, Kilmarii. Let us keep it that way. But why doesn't he stop and float?*

Kilmarii slid into the water, the harness wrapped around her arm. The water was warm and welcoming, and the sunlight penetrated deeply.

Balkii swam slowly, his massive head turning slightly to follow her movements.

Sharks, even ones that look like whales must keep moving to breathe. Balkii cannot stop for us to harness him. We must catch him in his harness, like we catch fish in our nets, Kilmarii explained to Kayko and the other knowers riding on the mental stream.

Kayko jumped into the water to help, maneuvering the straps steadily while Kilmarii adjusted the fit.

Pare and Ouray watched from the ship, as Ouray directed from above, *Looser at the dorsal fin! It needs to slide without chafing.*

Kayko adjusted the strap and raised his hand out of the water, in the direction of Kilmarii, *Try now.*

Kilmarii tested the harness, pulling it.

They were both being pulled around the ship by the circling Balkii. The enormous shark remained remarkably calm and accepted the harness, his great tail moving slowly.

It is good. We can secure it when it's time, Kayko confirmed.

Kayko and Kilmarii completed the latches on each side, and then released the harness. As the harness was being hoisted back up on deck, they swam to the rope ladder to climb back up to the deck.

Kayko clapped Kilmarii on the shoulder. "You did it."

Kilmarii's smile was brief but genuine. "We did it."

The moment of triumph was interrupted by the sound of the other ships preparing to leave. Kayko's smile faltered as he realized their time together was coming to an end.

The clan gathered to say their goodbyes. Kilmarii and Kayko stood apart from the crowd, their hands locked.

Kayko swallowed hard. *It will be strange to be without you.*

Kilmarii tried to speak aloud but hesitated. She wanted him to hear the words that were in her heart.

Kayko's shoulders sagged slightly before he straightened. "When I see you again, I will take you to the highlands and show you all the places I have shared with you."

Kilmarii tilted her head down so that he would

not see her tears forming, *I am curious to see this place.*

He nodded, and a small smile broke through his sadness. "You will learn to ride a horse. I will show you how we grow crops and hunt. You will see another way of life. A different part of our clan."

Kilmarii's eyes swelled over with tears forming. "I would like that."

Kayko did not hesitate; he pulled her into a quick embrace. "Stay safe."

"You too," Kilmarii whispered, her voice steady, despite the ache in her chest.

As Kayko boarded the departing vessel bound to Maleia's ship, he turned back and raised his arm above his head.

"Aho, Kilmarii!" he shouted.

Tozi and Jyukan stood at the rail beside him. They continued to watch as Ouray's vessel grew smaller.

Kilmarii turned away from them and took her position on deck, her thoughts reaching out to say a quiet goodbye.

You'll be alright, Jyukan sent reassuringly. *You have Ouray, and try not to get into more trouble.*

As the horizon swallowed the three vessels, Ouray rested a hand on Kilmarii's shoulder. "They'll make it back safely," he said aloud, his voice firm.

Kilmarii nodded, her eyes still lingering on the empty expanse. "And so will we."

Pare set down a large leather bag and joined

them at the rail. She asked, "The whale shark harness is ready and will pull well, but how long will the whale shark need to rest? When should we anchor?"

"Whale sharks are slow swimmers, but they never stop swimming for sleep."

The shocked look on Pare's and Ouray's faces amused Kilmarii. "I see that I have taught you something new."

As his eyes perused the vast, open water, Ouray proposed, "When we reach the ocean, we will sail day and night, but for the rest of today and tonight we will stay in the bay, so we may become well adapted to traveling by Balkii power."

Pare departed to share the news with the rest of the clan on board.

Kilmarii watched Balkii's shadow beneath the surface; her connection to the great creature grew stronger with every passing moment.

This journey, she knew, would be one of trust—between her and Balkii, between her and the rest of the clan. The days ahead would test her resolve, and she felt ready.

The crew moved efficiently, checking ropes and preparing for the night's meal. Kilmarii found Ouray sitting up in his sleeping deck, leaning against the rail, gazing out over the horizon where the first stars had begun to emerge. She climbed up the wall ladder and sat beside him, her posture straight, her eyes scanning the same distant point.

Kilmarii The Wayfinder

"This will be a long journey," Ouray said reflectively. "We have enough supplies for the people on board, but the armadillos will need fresh food. Their strength is important for the task ahead."

Kilmarii nodded thoughtfully. "Will we stop to gather herbs as well?"

Ouray's lips curved into a small smile. "Yes, that too. Herbs are the foundation of so much healing."

Kilmarii's gaze drifted to the deck where the armadillos rested, their small forms curled up in the corner.

"This long journey… it means I will have time to learn from you."

Ouray turned his head toward her, his expression warm, "Indeed. I will share with you what I know. How to read memories, how to understand their layers and their truths. And I will teach you the medicine methods passed down in our family."

Her expression brightened, a flicker of excitement broke through her usual demeanor, and the child inside reemerged.

Ouray studied her for a moment, his smile deepening. "Before we leave the bay and head out to the ocean, I will ask something of you."

"Anything," Kilmarii replied with sincerity, her voice resolute.

"Take me to the Temple of the Water," he said, his voice low but filled with purpose. "I have heard much from you, Kayko, Tozi, and Jyukan about what it did for them. I need to feel it for myself. I wish to heal my legs."

Kilmarii placed her hands around his arm, then moved gently to rest her forehead against his chest.

"See for yourself," she said softly, closing her eyes and opening her mind fully to him.

Ouray's brow furrowed as he was welcomed into the vivid stream of memories she offered. He saw the crystalline waters, the glowing cave, the spiraling stone at its entrance. He felt the pull of the tide, the power in the rising bubbles, the overwhelming presence of something ancient and alive.

When the vision faded, his expression was unreadable for a long moment until he finally lifted his eyes to hers, "Will you keep the sharks from attacking us if we enter the cave?"

Kilmarii nodded, her eyes still closed. "Yes, it is easy," she said, her voice a whisper. "But the waters flow in and out of the tide pool; perhaps we can use those waters to receive the blessings of the temple to change you…and the others who wish for it."

Ouray's hand moved to her shoulder, resting there lightly. "Then we will go together. We will bathe in the tide pool of the Temple of the Water."

She opened her eyes and stared into his eyes, her resolve mirrored in his. She reflected, "We should go during the low tide when the current is less dangerous."

Kilmarii The Wayfinder

Chapter Thirty-Two

A Great Hope

Pare stood at the ship's edge, her voice steady but edged with urgency, "Lower the vessels. We must take the first shift before the tide changes again." She gestured to the crew, who moved quickly, the ropes creaking as they lowered the wooden boats into the sea.

Kilmarii took her place in the first vessel, her bare feet braced against the damp wood as she steadied herself. Ouray gripped the frame, his knuckles whitening, as two men carefully lowered him into the boat. His legs hung lifelessly, a reminder of why he had come.

Behind them, the second small vessel followed. Soft laughter and prayers drifted across the water as the clan members prepared themselves to enter the

Kilmarii The Wayfinder

tide pool of the Temple of the Water. The rhythmic pulse of the tide accompanied their journey, a steady heartbeat beneath the calls of circling seabirds.

As they approached the tide pool, the carved stone at the entrance of the cave loomed large. The spirals carved in the stone gleamed slick with seawater, and the pool itself shimmered with an unearthly glow, as if alive. Kilmarii was the first to step out; her toes sank into the wet black sand.

"Be mindful of the current," she warned as she turned to assist the others out of the vessel. Two men lifted Ouray from the vessel, their movements careful and deliberate to keep him from harm.

Ouray's breathing quickened as he was lowered into the water; the warm, invigorating tide lapping gently at his thighs. His hands trembled as he touched the surface, feeling its vitality.

"When will it begin?" he asked, his voice trembling with emotion.

"For Kayko and me, it was the next morning," she said, reassuringly. "For Tozi and Jyukan, it was shown over two days and nights."

Around them, other clan members entered the pool, their faces glowing with anticipation. Some sat quietly, their eyes closed in prayer or contemplation. Others, overcome by the joy of the moment, splashed and played like children, their laughter a sacred offering at the entrance of the temple.

Pare sat next to Ouray, her hand resting

protectively on her belly.

The atmosphere was charged with optimism, the moment a rare reprieve for the hardworking clan. With the success of their recent trade and the promise of renewal, the tide pool became more than just a place of healing—it became a symbol of hope and possibility.

As the tide shifted and the glow of the tide pool began to fade with the waning light. Kilmarii and Pare rose from the water in unison. The last of the clan members reluctantly climbed back onto the vessels, their laughter and hushed conversations carried on the salt-tinged breeze. The dolphins, sensing the end of their task, gathered around, their smooth bodies cutting through the waves with effortless grace.

"Back to the ship," Pare called, her voice ringing out firm and clear.

The dolphins pulled the small vessels swiftly over the now-receding waters, their harnesses taut as the sea reflected the deepening hues of twilight.

When they reached the whale ship, the clan members helped each other aboard. Gripping their arms for support, Ouray was carefully lifted by two men.

On the deck, movement stirred as the Esors moved toward their tasks once more. One stepped forward.

The Esor named Kryn, spoke directly to Kilmarii, "I will assist you in harnessing the whale shark for the journey."

Kilmarii The Wayfinder

Kilmarii crossed her arms dismissively, "That's a task for a Yutki to do. The whale sharks are massive, unpredictable. It requires precision."

Kryn met her gaze without flinching, "Kayko was your only Yutki, and he left on a ship. Watch, and you'll see an Esor can handle it just as well." Kryn grasped Kilmarii's hand and placed it on her forehead.

Scanning her mind, Kilmarii quickly realized that Kryn possessed the mind of a Nek and the skills equal to those of any clan member, Yutki or otherwise. She had apprenticed as a Yutki before such a title existed, and she had trained under Ouray and Tozi.

Is she a half-sister of Ouray's? Kilmarii wondered, *No.... perhaps she is Mato's child?*

"I apologize for my error," Kilmarii implored. "I will call the whale shark under the ship. And you and your partner will secure the harness together."

A confident Kilmarii closed her eyes and called the whale shark to come under the ship and glide into his harness.

The clan gathered at the railings as Kryn and three other Esors moved efficiently in the ocean waters at the front of the ship, stretching out the harnesses over the water. The sea churned as the massive silhouette of the whale shark glided closer, its speckled skin glistening under the fading sunlight.

Kryn steadied herself, her focus unbroken as the whale shark began to enter the harness. "Hold position," she commanded the others. The Esors work seamlessly, securing the harness with ease.

The lines were tightened, and the harness was checked one final time before climbing back on the deck. Their faces marked with quiet satisfaction.

The tension aboard the ship was palpable until Kryn raised her hand to grab the rope ladder. "It's done," she called out.

With the whale shark secured, the ship lurched slightly as it turned northwest, following the currents toward the open ocean.

The clan settled into their routines, the earlier joy from the tide pool still lingering on their expressions.

Kilmarii stood at the bow, the stars spread across the sky. The ship sailed onward, carrying secrets and promises.

Kilmarii The Wayfinder

A note from Professor Asil Wysong:

"It is my pleasure to announce that I have been granted a series of guest lectures next semester. I look forward to sharing more stories of my Yutki ancestors."

Lisa Newton

ABOUT THE AUTHOR

Lisa A. Newton, M.Ed.
International Best-Selling Author

Lisa Newton has co-authored four Amazon best-selling spiritual self-help e-books and one international best-selling e-book.

She is a career educator who specializes in teaching language arts to students with specific learning challenges and students who are multi-language learners.

Her career accomplishments include writing and designing three virtual secondary English courses.

The Kilmarii book series will cover the life of the main character.

www.ingramcontent.com/pod-product-compliance
Lightning Source LLC
Chambersburg PA
CBHW060548260626
47161CB00003B/1102